The Haunted Carousel

Where had Ned gone? Nancy could hear running footsteps somewhere in the distance, but it was hard to judge where the sound was coming from. She could only plunge forward, zigzagging among the concessions, hoping to catch a glimpse of her vanished friend.

At first, she had been reluctant to call out his name, for fear of alerting the sinister prowlers. But as her worries grew for his safety, Nancy threw caution to the wind and shouted, "Ned! Can you hear me? Where are you?"

As she rounded the corner her heart flew into her mouth. She almost stumbled over something bulky, something barely visible in the semi-darkness, lying on the ground. At that moment someone switched on the overhead lights of the midway. Nancy gasped: It was Ned, sprawled motionless on the ground!

Nancy Drew
Mystery Stories

Available from MINSTREL Books

NANCY DREW®

THE HAUNTED CAROUSEL

CAROLYN KEENE

A MINSTREL® BOOK

PUBLISHED BY POCKET BOOKS

New York   London   Toronto   Sydney   Tokyo   Singapore

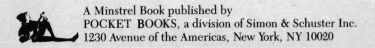 A Minstrel Book published by
POCKET BOOKS, a division of Simon & Schuster Inc.
1230 Avenue of the Americas, New York, NY 10020

ISBN: 0-671-66227-9

First Minstrel Books printing April 1988

10 9 8 7 6 5 4 3 2

NANCY DREW, NANCY DREW MYSTERY STORIES,
A MINSTREL BOOK and colophon are registered trademarks
of Simon & Schuster Inc.

Cover art by Aleta Jenks

Printed in the U.S.A.

Contents

THE HAUNTED
CAROUSEL

1

Mystery Challenge

"Can we see the haunted carousel, Nancy?!"

"Of course! That's where we're going now, Billy," Nancy Drew assured the excited little boy.

Nancy and her two friends, Bess Marvin and George Fayne, were taking the three small Custer children—relatives of Bess and George—through the amusement-park area of green, wooded Riverside Park.

"Why is the merry-go-round haunted?" asked Billy's seven-year-old sister, wide-eyed.

"Well, that's a bit of a mystery, Janet."

"And maybe you're just the person to solve it, Miss Drew!" called out a voice on Nancy's right.

1

The titian-haired teenager turned and saw a rangy young man in a summer sports jacket striding toward her. Nancy recognized him as Rick Jason, a reporter for the River Heights *News*.

"Is that an invitation?" she smiled.

"Call it a challenge!" Jason shot back.

Several times recently, in the middle of the night when the park was closed, the carousel had suddenly lit up and begun playing music and turning around. Each time, when people came running to investigate, the carousel would stop and go dark again. The spooky incidents had attracted wide interest, and many wild guesses were being made about the cause.

"When I take on a mystery case," Nancy told the reporter, "it's usually to help someone. I don't believe I've ever tackled a mystery on a dare before." Her blue eyes twinkled. "Can you give me one good reason why I should accept your challenge?"

"I'll give you two. First—you're the most successful sleuth in or around River Heights— maybe in this part of the country."

Nancy blushed. "Flattery will get you nowhere, Mr. Jason!"

"Don't be so modest, Nan—he's right," spoke up George Fayne, a slim girl with short, dark hair.

2

The praise was well earned. Daughter of Carson Drew, a prominent River Heights attorney, Nancy had displayed an unusual knack for solving mysteries. Her father frequently made use of her talent in connection with his own law cases, and her feats of detection had often been reported on television and in the newspapers.

"Second," Rick Jason went on, "I'll see if I can get the *News* to put up a reward. You name it, and I'll try to talk the managing editor and publisher into going along. The story should be worth it—especially if you can come up with a solution!"

"Hm." Nancy reflected. "Then how about offering every boy and girl in River Heights a bus trip to the park and an afternoon of free fun-rides?"

"You're on!" said Rick.

Nancy dimpled and they shook hands. Then the reporter whipped out a camera and snapped several pictures of the pretty young sleuth.

"Oh, how exciting!" gushed plump, blond Bess Marvin as the girls and their three little charges walked on. Rick Jason had hurried off to file his story. "You'll have everyone in town breathlessly following the progress of your investigation!"

"That's what I'm afraid of," Nancy quipped wryly. She paused a moment later, glancing off to one side with a look of concern. "Isn't that the Swiss couple we met at the cotton-candy stand?"

"Yes, it's the Trompels," said George. "I wonder what's wrong?"

The three girls had gotten into conversation with the young couple while waiting to be served. They learned that Konrad and Judi Trompel had arrived in New York only two days before to begin an early planned tour of the U.S.A. River Heights and Riverside Park were their first stop outside the huge sky-scraper metropolis.

But something had evidently gone wrong. Trudi was weeping while her husband tried to comfort her. Nancy went up to them.

"Can we help?" she asked sympathetically.

"I doubt it, but thank you, anyhow," said Konrad Trompel. "I am afraid only a policeman can help us."

"Are you in trouble?"

"Yes, I have just discovered my wallet has been stolen."

"You mean here in the park?"

"So it seems. I had it only a little while ago, when we were talking at the cotton-candy stand. But now it is gone—snatched by some pickpocket, no doubt."

Konrad explained ruefully that the wallet contained all the money they possessed—partly in American dollars and partly in Swiss francs—which meant that they would have to cut short their vacation and return to Switzerland.

Bess and George were shocked and embarrassed that two foreign visitors, especially two as nice as Trudi and Konrad Trompel, should have been victims of such a heartless crime while visiting River Heights. While her friends sympathized with the unhappy couple, Nancy—who knew a good deal about the ways of criminals—decided to offer her own help as a detective.

"Did anyone bump you recently?" she asked Konrad.

The young Swiss looked surprised at her question. "Why yes, a man bumped into me just as we stopped to get a drink at the water fountain."

"Can you remember what he looked like?"

"Of course. He was a heavyset man—going bald, I believe—and he had on a checked suit. But why do you ask?"

"Because that's probably when you were robbed." Nancy told Konrad that pickpockets often work in teams. When the burly man bumped him to distract his attention, another crook—a light-fingered "dip," skilled at picking pockets—had doubtless seized the chance to lift Konrad's wallet.

The dip, Nancy went on, would have passed the wallet to a third crook, who would quickly strip it of its valuable contents and dump the empty wallet in the nearest trash bin. "That way," she added, "it's almost impossible to catch any member of the team with incriminating evidence on him, unless they're nabbed within moments of the crime."

Konrad sighed. "Then there is little hope of recovering our money, eh?"

"There may be a chance in this case," Nancy said thoughtfully. "Anyhow, let's not give up just yet. The first thing is to find where they threw your wallet."

The young sleuth suggested that they check the trash baskets nearest the water fountain. Two baskets were soon located, in opposite directions from the fountain.

Eight-year-old Gary Custer gave a triumphant whoop after peering into the second basket. "I found it!" he yelled and held up a brown wallet.

Konrad confirmed that the wallet was his and thanked the little boy, even though the wallet was now empty of money. "At least I have my identification cards and driver's license back," he added gratefully.

"This is just the first step," Nancy responded. Gazing around, she saw a refreshment counter nearby and hurried toward it. "Did either of you see a person throw something into that trash basket just a few minutes ago?" she asked the two counter attendants.

One shook his head. "Sorry, I didn't notice. Too busy dishing out hot dogs!"

But the other told Nancy, "Yeah, matter of fact I did see a guy throw something away there. I meant to go over and check, because it looked like a wallet."

"It *was* a wallet," said Nancy. "Can you remember what the fellow looked like?"

"Sure, he was about nineteen or twenty, with long, dark hair—and he had on a red polo shirt."

"Thanks!" Nancy beamed. "You've helped a lot."

The girl quickly mapped out a plan of action. She suggested that their group split up into four pairs and spread out through the amusement park, looking for the burly, balding man in the checked suit or the young man in the red polo shirt. Bess, George, and Nancy herself would each take one of the Custer children, while the Trompels would stay together.

"I'm sure there's a team of at least three pickpockets working together," Nancy added. "If we can find either of the two suspects, he may lead us to their partners in crime."

Within ten minutes, little Janet Custer came running up to Nancy, who had Janet's younger brother Billy by the hand. "George and I found one of the crooks!" the little girl cried excitedly.

"Which one?" asked Nancy.

"The bald-headed one!"

Nancy quickly rounded up the Trompels, Bess, and Gary, and they all rejoined George Fayne, who pointed out a thickset figure in a checked suit. The man was waiting near the park's shooting gallery.

"You are right! That is the man who bumped me!" Konrad declared in a low, intense voice.

Even as he spoke, the balding crook was joined by another man—an elderly, skinny fellow with a wrinkled, pinched-looking face.

"I'll bet *he*'s the dip who picked your pocket," Nancy conjectured. "They're probably waiting for their partner in the red shirt to come and split the loot, since he's the one who actually took the money from your wallet."

Since Nancy's group were partly screened by shrubbery, the two crooks did not yet realize

8

they were being watched. She urged her companions to run and look for a policeman, while she herself kept the suspects under surveillance.

Within minutes, her prediction was borne out as a tall, slender young man in a red polo shirt came walking toward the two older crooks. Nancy cast about frantically, hoping to glimpse a park policeman. But none was in sight.

If I don't do something fast, she fretted, they'll get away!

In desperation, Nancy decided that her best move would be to try to catch the young crook alone before he joined forces with his two partners. She might at least be able to recover the Trompels' money, even though it meant giving up any chance of bringing the pickpockets to justice.

Nancy hurried across the grass and confronted the young man in the red polo shirt while he was still some distance from his two confederates.

"Hand over that money you stole!" she demanded boldly.

His face seemed to come all apart in a look of stunned dismay. "Wh-what do you mean?"

"You know very well what I mean! I'm talking about the money you stripped from that stolen wallet, just before you tossed it in a trash basket."

Seeing his expression of guilt and growing alarm, Nancy pressed on sternly. "You can be identified as the thief because part of that money is in Swiss francs. If you surrender the loot now, I'll let you go. But you'd better hand it over fast," she stated, "because if you don't, you'll soon find yourself behind bars!"

The young thief hesitated and gulped fearfully. But a moment later, his expression hardened into a mocking grin. Glancing over her shoulder, Nancy at once saw why. The burly, balding crook and his skinny cohort were hurrying toward them with angry scowls and doubled-up fists.

"Beat it, lady!" the bigger one bellowed.

2

The Wonderland Gallop

Nancy tried not to show her fear. But she could tell from the looks on their faces that the two oncoming crooks were deadly serious. If they could not scare her off, the bigger one was ready to use force!

Should she stand her ground or run? Nancy's heart was pounding, and her throat suddenly felt dry. If she stayed, she might be hurt. But to give up now meant the Trompels would lose all their money and have to return to Switzerland, their American vacation ruined by these vicious, unfeeling criminals.

If only help would come! Nancy bit her lip to keep it from trembling and decided to stall for time, at least for a few moments longer.

Suddenly, the shrill blast of a police whistle split the air! Then came the faint sound of George's voice calling, "We're coming, Nancy!"

The two older members of the pickpocket gang skidded to a halt only a second before they would have reached Nancy. Both glanced over their shoulders toward the sound of the whistle.

The burly crook's face twisted with rage as he saw himself lose both his loot and chance for revenge. Then he and his scrawny companion turned and fled!

Nancy boldly reached out and grabbed the red-shirted youth's forearm. "See how your pals have deserted you?" she exclaimed scornfully. "Better give up that money you stole while you still have a chance!"

The young crook wavered, his face pale and oozing perspiration. With an oath, he jerked free of Nancy's grasp. At the same time, he grabbed a wad of bills from his pocket and tossed them into the air. Then he, too, turned and ran!

George and the park policeman reached the scene within moments. "Oh, Nancy! Thank goodness we got here in time!" George said breathlessly.

The officer didn't even stop, but just pounded on in pursuit of the fleeing crooks.

Meanwhile, the breeze was scattering the money. Nancy and George were hastily collecting it when the Trompels, Bess, and the three Custer children came hurrying up. Everyone joined in the scramble, and soon they had retrieved all the money.

"Better count it," Nancy advised Konrad Trompel.

Trudi was crying quietly, but this time the tears were from relief. "Oh, Miss Drew, you're an angel! How can we ever thank you enough?"

"The money is all here," Konrad told his wife with a happy smile. Then he shook Nancy's hand earnestly. "God bless you, Miss Drew— and all the rest of you, my friends. Trudi and I are more grateful than we can say. You cannot imagine how bad we felt when it seemed we would have to go back home at once without seeing your country. But now we will enjoy our American tour more than ever!"

The Trompels wanted to reward the girls and their small companions, but Nancy, Bess, and George would not hear of it. "We just want you to have a good vacation," Bess said, dimpling into her irrepressible, round-cheeked smile.

The young couple thought they should wait at the scene until the park officer returned.

"If the police need my testimony for any reason, they know where to reach me," Nancy told the Trompels. Then the three girls took the Custer children and walked on to the carousel.

Its gay music filled the air. The three children were jumping up and down in their eagerness to ride the merry-go-round.

Just as they reached it, the carousel stopped. Gary ran forward, shouting, "I want the black horse!" Janet and Billy also found steeds to their liking. Bess and George helped the two little ones on while Nancy bought the tickets. Then the three teenagers went over to a park bench facing the merry-go-round and sat down to watch as it started up again.

The carousel was certainly a beauty, with flashing mirrors and gilt cupids and other ornate decorations. Its name, *Wonderland Gallop*, was painted on the metal canopy in fancy gold-and-red letters. The horses looked spirited and realistic and were beautifully painted.

"Golly, I remember how much I loved to ride them!" Bess reminisced. "You did too, Nancy."

"So did I," George put in with a laugh, "but my favorite ride was always the rollercoaster!"

While her chums were talking, Nancy was watching the operator of the merry-go-round. A dark-haired man with a lined face and a mustache, he looked about fifty years old. He had a tow-headed young assistant, who collected the tickets and helped the children off the horses when the ride was over.

The older man left his assistant in charge and began walking toward a refreshment stand. Nancy intercepted him and introduced herself. "You're the owner of the carousel, Mr., uh . . ."

"Novak," he said. "Leo Novak. Yes, I'm the owner. What can I do for you?"

Nancy explained that she had been challenged by a reporter to find out why the carousel turned on so spookily at night of its own accord. "Can you suggest any possible cause?"

Leo Novak shook his head. "Beats me. The whole thing's weird. I've checked over the motor, the operating machinery—everything. I can't find anything out of order."

"Could someone just be playing a prank?"

Novak shrugged. "Search me. It's possible, I suppose, but don't ask me who or how."

"Hm." Nancy frowned thoughtfully. "Mr. Novak, you just moved the carousel back to this park recently, didn't you?"

"That's right. The *Wonderland Gallop* used to run right here in Riverside Park up till about eight years ago. Then old Mr. Ogden, the first

15

owner, moved it to another park out in the Midwest."

"Were you with the carousel then?"

"Yep, I worked for Mr. Ogden for a long time. When he died, I bought it."

"Why did you move it back here?"

"Oh, the place where we were was getting pretty run-down and seedy—business was falling off—so I decided it was time to find a better location. Besides, I always liked River Heights."

"Do you think anything could have happened to the operating machinery, or anyone could have tampered with it, while the carousel was being moved?" Nancy probed persistently.

"Nah. Anyhow, like I say, I checked the whole setup when it started acting funny, and I couldn't find any bugs." Novak spread his hands helplessly. "Just one of those crazy things, I guess."

"How strange." Nancy smiled. "Well, thank you for your help, Mr. Novak."

"Anytime, Miss Drew. And good luck with your spook hunting!"

Nancy rejoined Bess and George and the children, and they resumed their ramble through the park. After sampling the Monster, the Dodgems, the Ferris wheel, the Log Jam, and then, much to the delight of the three little

Custers, the Haunted House, George looked at the other two teenagers and sighed, "Wow, I give up. I'm bushed."

"Anyhow," her cousin Bess pointed out, "it's time for dinner."

As Nancy and George laughed, the plump girl—who was often teased about her appetite —blushed but chuckled good-naturedly. "Well, it is. And remember, we have to cook it on the houseboat."

Bess and George's uncle, Mr. Custer, had rented the houseboat during his vacation from his office job and had come downriver on it with his family to visit their relatives in River Heights. Tonight Bess and George were to stay with the three children on the boat while their parents dined with the Faynes and Marvins.

"Come on, Nancy! You've got to see the boat to believe it. It's such fun to live on," George said.

"You bet!" little Janet chimed in. "I wish we could live on it all the time."

"Yeah, it's great," her brother Gary added.

While they chatted, the group was walking out of the amusement-ride area and through the adjoining woodland on their way to the marina at the edge of Riverside Park. As they approached the dock in the late-afternoon sunshine, Janet burst out, "Look, there's someone on our boat! . . . It's a man!"

Wide-eyed, the girls saw a figure silhouetted against the lowering sun. As they watched, he disappeared on the other side of the houseboat.

"I'll go for help," Bess said nervously.

"All right. And you three stay here, please, while George and I see what's going on," Nancy told the Custers. She picked up a small but hefty rock, while George found a broken tree branch.

Determinedly, the two girls began to walk out on the dock toward the houseboat, their hearts pounding!

3

Night Watch

The deck of the houseboat lay almost on a level with the dock. As they reached the craft, George shot a quizzical glance at Nancy, who put a finger to her lips. Then both girls stepped aboard.

With her lips close to George's ear, Nancy whispered that she would tiptoe around the bow of the boat, while George went around the stern. "That way," she added, "we'll close in on him from two directions at once, and he won't be able to deal with both of—"

Nancy broke off with a start as a masculine voice suddenly shouted, *"Boo!"*

George screamed and clutched her friend. Nancy whirled around. Both girls shrieked,

"Ned!" at the sight of a tall, husky young man in a Western shirt and jeans, who had just leaped out at them from around a corner of the cabin. He was Nancy's boyfriend, Ned Nickerson.

Seeing how startled the girls were, he put an arm around each of them reassuringly and apologized, "Sorry—I didn't really mean to scare the wits out of you." When he noticed the rock and tree branch they were clutching, Ned chuckled. "Guess I'm the one who should have been scared. It might've been lights out if I'd gotten beaned with one of those!"

When he had met the three little Custer children, and he and Nancy had been shown all over the houseboat, Ned said, "Actually, I didn't just come down here to play bogeyman, Nancy. I went to your house first, and Hannah said I might find you here at the marina."

Bess, who had happily rejoined her friends after seeing who the intruder was, cut in, "Well, now that you're here, you can stay and have dinner with us!"

Ned, who had brown eyes and wavy, dark hair, replied with his usual ready smile. "It's good of you to invite me after I played such a trick, but I really came to ask Nancy if she could switch our date from tomorrow night to tonight."

Turning to his friend, he added, "You see, I have to make a quick trip back to Emerson College to straighten out my program for the fall semester. There's been a computer mixup on the courses I signed up for."

"Oh, tonight will be fine, Ned," Nancy told him.

"Well, you two are still welcome to stay," George said with a mischievous grin, "but if I were you, Nancy, I wouldn't."

Even Bess burst out laughing. "Neither would I, if you want the truth—especially because *I* know what we'll be cooking tonight!"

"I made reservations at the Rustlers' Inn," Ned said when the laughter died down, "but if—"

"Say no more," Nancy interrupted hastily. "Just lead the way!"

In his own car, Ned trailed Nancy's back to the Drew house, so she could change.

"Gee, you look great just as you are, Nancy," he protested as she started upstairs. "Everyone goes to the Rustlers' Inn in jeans."

"I know, but I'd like to get a little more Western-looking," Nancy responded with a chuckle. "And I want to freshen up a bit, too."

A short time later, having changed into a blue-and-white checkered shirt and tied a red

21

bandana around her neck, Nancy picked up her small shoulder bag and announced, "Ta-da! I'm ready."

Ned looked her over approvingly and grinned. "Guess I should've worn my Western boots!"

At the inn, over thick, sizzling steaks, Nancy told Ned how reporter Rick Jason had challenged her to solve the mystery of the haunted carousel.

"I read about that in the newspaper," Ned murmured, taking a forkful of crisp, green salad.

"There must be some perfectly natural explanation, and I intend to find it," Nancy declared. "But first I'd like to see it happen with my own eyes."

"Do you have any plan?"

"Well, I thought I might keep watch on the park tonight."

"What if nothing happens?" Ned asked. "The carousel doesn't go into its spooky routine every night, does it?"

"No, you're right," Nancy admitted. "Unless I'm lucky, I may have to stake out the park several nights in a row. You wouldn't want to join me on watch tonight, by any chance?"

"Wild horses couldn't keep me away! What's more, I want you to promise me something."

"What's that?" Nancy's blue eyes twinkled.

"That you'll never go there late at night, un-less I'm in River Heights so I can go with you," Ned said earnestly. "Okay?"

"Well . . . perhaps you're right," Nancy said as they started their apple pie and coffee. Ned didn't realize that she had actually promised nothing.

Later, after deciding on the best time to ar-rive at Riverside Park, Ned and Nancy left the restaurant and drove to a movie theater that was showing a horror film they had chosen to see. It had gotten rave reviews as a spine-chilling thril-ler.

Two hours later, when the movie ended, they walked out of the theater laughing.

"It wasn't really very scary, did you think, Ned?"

"Nope. Out of two hours' playing time, there were about two minutes of shock. The rest was silly."

Laughing, they linked arms and sauntered to Ned's car.

"I'd like to stop home first and tell Dad where we're going," Nancy said. "And maybe pick up a sweater, too. Shall I bring one of Dad's for you to wear, Ned?"

"Thanks, but I have one in the car, Nancy. It

might be a good idea to take along some night glasses, though. We can pick them up at my house on our way to the park."

"You mean binoculars?"

"Right. Mine are good for low-light and night surveillance. They're used by the navy and coast guard," Ned replied.

Carson Drew was reading in his usual comfortable armchair in the living room when they arrived.

"Well! Good to see you, Ned. Enjoy the movie, honey?" He gave Nancy a hug.

"Mildly, Dad," Nancy said, smiling at Ned. Then she told her father about the latest mystery she had undertaken to solve. "So, if it's okay with you, Ned and I are going to the park tonight to see if the carousel goes on again when everything's dark."

The distinguished attorney had long since learned to trust his daughter's good judgment and quick-witted ability to deal with emergencies. "Very well," he nodded. "If Ned's with you, I won't worry. But you two be careful!"

Nancy changed into a pair of sturdy casual shoes, then grabbed a sweater and an extra flashlight and left the house with Ned. The two stopped at his house to pick up the special

24

binoculars before driving on to the park. It was about ten minutes to eleven when they reached their destination.

"I think we'd better park the car in the public parking lot near the marina and walk back," Ned remarked. "What do you think, Nancy?"

"Good idea. It'll be less conspicuous there after the park closes."

Closing time for the amusement area of Riverside Park was eleven o'clock. Customers were drifting out as Nancy and Ned approached, and the rides were shutting down, one by one.

The amusement section was fenced off from the rest of the wooded park by a pipe-and-chain barrier. Nancy and Ned stayed outside this barrier and made their way along a darkened footpath to a clump of trees and shrubbery that afforded a clear view of the carousel.

"Let's wait in there," Nancy suggested.

The carousel was situated near the side of the park that overlooked the riverbank. Its lights were still on as the teenage sleuth and her companion made themselves comfortable in the hiding place she had chosen. The proprietor was busy counting his receipts for the evening, while his young assistant swept the platform and picked up candy wrappers and other debris with a spike.

Nancy lounged on the grass and Ned leaned against a tree trunk, watching the amusement-park area grow dark as the lights were turned off one by one.

Meanwhile, the carousel operator's young assistant finished his chores, called good night to his boss, and left the park. A few minutes later, Leo Novak turned off the merry-go-round lights, and the two watchers saw him trudge off toward his trailer, which was parked near a few other vans and campers in which lived other park concessionaires.

Finally, all was dark.

"How long do you want to wait, Nancy?" Ned found himself speaking in a hushed voice.

"I think if nothing has happened by—oh, say, one-thirty, we may as well leave. From what I've heard and read in the news reports, the carousel has never started up later than that."

They sat quietly and watched and waited. It was a lovely, starlit night and, with the crickets chirping, very peaceful. Nancy's eyelids grew heavier minute by minute, and began to close.

Suddenly, Ned nudged her awake. "Did you see something move over there?" he whispered, reaching for his binoculars.

Nancy's eyes widened quickly. "Yes! . . . Look, Ned!"

Even without the night glasses, she could make out two dark figures heading toward the carousel. They stepped up on the outer edge of the merry-go-round, and Nancy saw them dimly silhouetted by a small glow of light, as if a flashlight had been turned on. After pausing for a moment, they began moving from horse to horse.

"What the dickens are they up to?" Ned grumbled. "It's hard to see with their backs turned."

He handed the binoculars to Nancy. As she focused on the two intruders, they stopped and now appeared to be centering their interest on one particular horse.

An instant later, Nancy caught her breath as the lights of the carousel suddenly blazed on! Organ music churned loudly and the merry-go-round began to revolve!

4

Danger in the Dark

Nancy and Ned gaped in amazement. The effect was almost as if the carousel had magically come alive in the middle of the night!

"What happened?" Ned exclaimed. "Did those two spooks start it up?"

"No, they weren't even near the controls! In fact, they almost fell off when the merry-go-round started turning! I think they were caught by surprise—and scared! Here, see for yourself, Ned!"

Nancy handed him the binoculars. By now, a few lights were coming on in the park trailers as the carousel music blared out through the night stillness.

The two dark figures abruptly fled!

"I'm going after them!" Ned blurted. He sprang to his feet, leaped across the chain barrier enclosing the amusement area, and headed in pursuit. Nancy followed close behind.

The two mysterious intruders were running away from the carousel in the opposite direction from Ned and Nancy's stakeout position. So far, the only lights in the park were those turned on in the campers and trailers belonging to the concessionaires and ride operators. Already, the two fugitives were disappearing in the darkness.

Nancy paused for a moment as Leo Novak came running up. Evidently, he had dressed in haste and had not even taken time to pull on a jacket or other top over his undershirt.

He looked both startled and angry, but his eyes widened in surprise on seeing the pretty teenager. "Where did you come from?" he demanded.

"A friend and I were keeping watch," she said briefly, "over there among the trees."

"See anything?

"Yes, two men came up to the carousel."

"Did they monkey with it?"

"I don't think so—at least not with the operating machinery. They seemed to be interested in the horses. But you'd better make sure everything's all right!"

Without bothering to explain further, Nancy resumed running after Ned and the two intruders. Her last glimpse of the boy had been as he veered off to the left, behind the Ferris wheel. But now he, too, was no longer in sight.

From the direction Ned had been heading, Nancy guessed that his pursuit of the fugitives must have taken him between the video-game arcade and a row of refreshment counters. She ran the same way.

Beyond loomed an array of booths, stands, and rides that made up the gaudy heart of the park's midway. Just now they were a maze of gloom and shadows.

Where had Ned gone? Nancy could hear running footsteps somewhere in the distance, but it was hard to judge the exact direction the sound was coming from. She could only plunge forward at random, zigzagging among the concessions, hoping to catch a glimpse of her vanished friend.

At first, she had been reluctant to call out his name, for fear of alerting the sinister prowlers. But as her worries grew for his safety, Nancy threw caution to the winds and shouted, "Ned!

. . . Ned, can you hear me? Where are you?"

Her heart flew into her mouth as she rounded the corner of a shuttered souvenir stand and almost stumbled over something lying on the ground. The obstacle, barely visible in the semi-darkness, felt bulky enough to be a human form.

At that moment, someone switched on the overhead lights of the midway. Nancy gasped in fear as she saw the figure at her feet. It was Ned, sprawled motionless on the ground!

"Oh, Ned—Ned!" she cried, dropping to one knee. "What happened?! Are you all right?!"

She turned him over and touched his forehead and cheek. He stirred, and his eyes opened. With a faint groan, Ned struggled to his feet. "Wow!" he muttered, rubbing the back of his head. "Someone must have conked me!"

"Maybe you'd better rest awhile," Nancy urged anxiously.

Ned gave her a quick hug and a sheepish grin. "Don't worry, I'm okay," he reassured her. "I don't think I was out more than a few seconds."

In any case, further pursuit seemed useless. After a quick circuit of the amusement-park area, the couple gave up their chase of the two intruders and returned to Ned's car.

31

Next morning, the young sleuth slept later than usual. When she came downstairs, a copy of the River Heights *News* was lying on the sofa. Nancy's eye was caught by her own picture on the front page. The accompanying story told how the famous girl detective had accepted the newspaper's challenge to solve the mystery of the haunted carousel.

"Oh, you've seen it already. I was going to show it to you, Nancy." Hannah Gruen, the Drews' motherly housekeeper, came into the living room from the kitchen, wiping her hands on her apron, and saw the teenager reading the newspaper article.

"Yes . . . my, it really puts me on the spot," Nancy commented ruefully.

"In more ways than one!" said Hannah. "Our phone's been ringing all morning. Thank goodness, it didn't wake you."

"Who was calling?"

"My goodness, I don't know. Some were cranks, I guess. Everybody wants to tell you how to solve the carousel mystery."

"Hannah, you should have put on the answering machine."

"That's just what I finally did, dear. Oh, wait a minute," the housekeeper added. "There was one sensible call—a girl who gave her name,

Joy Trent. She wants you to solve a private mystery for her."

Just then, there was a knock on the front screen door, and a familiar voice called in, "Nancy, it's me—Bess!"

"Oh, just a minute," Nancy said, getting up and going to the door.

The pretty girl looked bright-eyed and eager as she accompanied Nancy into the living room from the front hall. "What's going on?" she inquired keenly. "I tried to call you this morning, but I kept getting busy signals. I couldn't get through, so I came over to invite you to a cookout at my place tonight. Hello, Mrs. Gruen," Bess finished in a rush.

"How would you two like some breakfast?" the housekeeper responded with a twinkle. "Bess? Nancy?"

"Sounds good to me." Bess laughed. "Actually I did have a nibble when I first got up, but that was quite a while ago."

Nancy turned to the housekeeper. "Never mind, Hannah. We'll just pop into the kitchen and get something for ourselves."

After making themselves a leisurely breakfast of waffles with blueberry syrup and sausages and coffee, Bess and Nancy washed the dishes and made the kitchen tidy again.

"Bess, how would you like to come to the amusement park with me?" Nancy asked as she took off the apron she had donned for their dishwashing chore. "We won't be long. Then I'll drive you home."

"Sure, great."

On the way, Nancy told Bess of her and Ned's adventure in the park the night before.

"Oh, golly! Is Ned okay?" Bess inquired sympathetically.

"He seemed to be, thank heavens. Luckily he was only hit hard enough to stun him."

"Honestly, Nancy, you do get into the wildest adventures!"

The teenage sleuth chuckled. "Not on purpose, believe me—but at least that's better than getting bored, isn't it? Anyhow, that's why I'm going to the park. I'd like to see if I can find out what those two sneaks were doing on the carousel last night."

As noontime neared, the limited parking space outside the amusement-park entrance was already filling up with cars. So Nancy turned in to the nearby marina lot instead, as Ned had done the night before. Then she and Bess headed back on foot to the carousel.

Soon after they had entered the amusement-ride area, Bess nudged her companion and pointed off to the right. A park policeman was waving at them. "He's the one who went after those pickpockets yesterday!" the plump girl exclaimed.

"Yes, his name is Officer Doyle," Nancy murmured. "I wonder what's up? He looks like he wants to talk to us."

They met the policeman halfway. He was accompanied by a hard-jawed man in a gray suit, whom Nancy had never seen before.

"Say! You were mighty lucky yesterday, Nancy," Officer Doyle greeted the teenager. "Maybe you didn't realize it, but when you tangled with those crooks here in the park, you were really flirting with danger!"

5

The Lead Horse

"Flirting with danger?" Bess echoed, then turned to her friend, aghast. "Oh, Nancy!"

Even Nancy was taken aback. "Were they really that dangerous?" she asked Officer Doyle.

"They sure were! This gentleman here is Detective Mike Norris from the St. Louis Police Department. He can tell you all about them."

As Nancy flashed a quizzical smile at Doyle's companion, the park policeman suddenly realized that he had not yet introduced her properly. "Oh, sorry. Mike, if you haven't guessed already, this is Nancy Drew, a very clever young lady. She's mighty good at solving mysteries."

"And not bad at collaring pickpockets, either,

I hear." The detective grinned as he took Nancy's hand.

"Luckily, I had friends to help me, including Bess Marvin here," Nancy said modestly and introduced her companion to the two officers.

"One of those older crooks you saw yesterday was an escaped con named Fingers Malone," Detective Norris told the girls. "He was the little scrawny one. He's an expert dip and also a fugitive from the state penitentiary. He served twenty years of a twenty-five-year sentence. Then he broke out."

"Who was the big man?" Nancy asked. "He looked quite vicious."

"He is! His name's Baldy Krebs, and he's got a violent record. Fingers joined up with him after breaking out of the pen. They were almost caught at a park in St. Louis, but Krebs wounded the officer who tried to arrest them, and they got away."

"I take it they got away yesterday, too?" Nancy said to Officer Doyle.

He nodded regretfully. "Yes, I lost them outside the park. They split up. Krebs hopped on a passing bus and got away before I could signal the driver to stop. Malone gave me the slip by darting across the street through traffic."

Doyle added that after turning in his report at

37

the station house, he realized that the pair's description matched that of two wanted criminals, so the St. Louis Police Department was notified.

"And that's why you came here?" Nancy asked Detective Norris.

"Right. I just flew in this morning. Pickpockets usually operate in crowds, so we're hoping they may show up here at Riverside Park again."

Taking a couple of Wanted posters from his inside coat pocket, Norris unfolded them to show the two girls and went on, "With Krebs, of course, purse snatching and picking pockets are just a sideline—most of the crimes he's wanted for are more serious, like armed robbery. But Fingers Malone almost seems to have a fancy for amusement parks."

"Funny thing," Officer Doyle put in, "but this morning we got an anonymous phone tip by a caller who claimed to have seen Fingers and Baldy in Riverside Park, so that's another reason for believing they may be skulking around here again today."

"We'll keep our eyes open," Nancy promised.

"Well, we just wanted to warn you to be care-

38

ful. Have a good time, girls!" Both policeman smiled at Nancy and Bess and walked off.

The two girls sauntered on to the carousel. It was a lovely, warm summer day, and as they approached, the air was filled with the merry-go-round music and the shouts and laughter of the children riding the horses and other carved animals.

Leo Novak was nowhere in sight. His teen-age assistant was running the concession by himself. Nancy didn't bother speaking to him. She wanted time to inspect the horses slowly and without interruption.

"What are we looking for, Nancy?" Bess asked in a low voice.

"I really don't know. I'm not even sure which horses those fellows were examining last night, except that they were in the outer circle." The pretty young sleuth tapped her forefinger against her lips while thinking. "Guess we'll just have to look for anything unusual, or see if they show any sign of tampering."

"Okay, I'm going to take the other side of the merry-go-round." Bess turned and began walking around the whirling riders.

When the carousel stopped and the children had gotten off, both girls stepped onto the platform to examine the horses more closely. It was tedious, but soon they had looked over every mount in the outer circle. Neither girl had noticed anything out of the ordinary.

As Nancy stood deep in thought, someone came up to her and spoke. "Excuse me, but aren't you Miss Nancy Drew?"

Nancy looked up and saw a gray-haired man in a safari jacket. She nodded.

"I've read that you're investigating this haunted carousel mystery," he went on. "Please allow me to introduce myself. I'm Arno Franz."

Nancy accepted his handshake. After he had been introduced to Bess, Franz remarked, "I guess I look a little out of place among all you young people, but I love amusement parks. They're so bright and cheerful."

"I agree." Nancy smiled.

"Since I retired, I've traveled all over the country visiting them," Franz went on. "I'm what you might call an amusement-park buff. In fact I've thought about writing a book on them someday. I certainly have enough material."

"Really? If you ever do, let us know," Bess enthused. "Sounds like it would be fun to read!"

Nancy was struck by a thought. "Do you know much about carousels?"

"Well, I like to think I do. For instance, this one—the *Wonderland Gallop*—is quite old and still has the original carousel horses. Beautiful, aren't they?"

"How old are they?" Bess asked.

"Oh, they go back to the early 1920s, I would say—or perhaps even earlier than that," Arno Franz answered. "But did you notice that the lead horse is different in style from the others, which probably means it was a replacement?"

"Lead horse?" Nancy queried. "What do you mean?"

"That refers to the fanciest horse on the carousel, the one most ornately decorated."

"Oh yes, I see what you mean. They're all beautifully trimmed, but that black one does stand out."

"It's exquisite!" Bess agreed.

Not only did its trappings include flashing silver armor and a gold-painted harness, but its bridle and mane were decorated with rosebuds, and its saddle was bordered by carved cherubs.

"And yet in spite of all the fancy ornamentation," said Franz, "in some ways, it's not really as beautiful as the other horses. For instance, it's not as spirited-looking as a lead horse should be, and the outer surface is rather

41

smooth and uninteresting—I mean, it lacks the loving attention to detail that the carver lavished on the other horses."

"You're right. I hadn't noticed before, but I can see that, now that you point it out," Nancy said thoughtfully. "So if this is of different workmanship, it probably wasn't one of the original carousel animals?"

"Exactly." Franz nodded. "The wild idea occurred to me that at the time the lead horse was replaced, the carousel's operating machinery might have been tampered with."

"And that may explain why it turns on and shuts off by itself at night?"

"Right." The gray-haired man smiled and shrugged apologetically. "As I say, it's just a thought, but I figured I'd mention it."

"Thanks, I'm glad you did," Nancy responded. "It may be a clue worth following up."

After Arno Franz had said good-bye to the two girls, Nancy walked up to the youth who was running the merry-go-round and asked where she could find Leo Novak.

"He's probably in his trailer eating lunch," the assistant replied. "It's that blue-and-white one over there in the camping space among the trees . . . the one nearest the light pole."

Nancy thanked him for the information. Then

she and Bess walked over to the trailer which he had pointed out. Leo Novak answered on the first knock.

"Oh, it's you, Miss Drew," he said, recognizing the girl. "Find out anything new about what happened last night?"

"No, I was hoping that you might have." When Novak shook his head, Nancy went on, "Did you examine the carousel after I left you?"

"Yes, but there was nothing out of order."

"Hm." Nancy eyed the concessionaire reflectively. "Mr. Novak, I've been told that the lead horse on your carousel has evidently been replaced—that the one on there now is not the original."

Novak frowned. "Why yes, that's right," he answered slowly. "The lead horse got damaged and had to be replaced—a truck hauling trash out of the park skidded into it. But if you think that had anything to do with what happened last night, or any of the other nights, forget it. That truck accident occurred several years ago. But this spooky on-and-off stuff at night only began very recently."

"I see." Nevertheless, Nancy was still not willing to ascribe the weird phenomenon to ghostly causes. Whatever the explanation, she was convinced that *something* must have been done to the operating machinery to make the carousel turn on and off, apparently by itself. "Mr. Novak, would you permit me to have an engineer check out the carousel?"

Leo Novak hesitated, then shrugged his shoulders grudgingly. "Well, okay. This whole spooky business is a pain in the neck!"

"Thanks, Mr. Novak. It won't cost you a thing," Nancy told him. "Good-bye for now."

Nancy and Bess walked back along the midway, heading for the park exit. Suddenly, Nancy gasped as she saw a skinny figure in the distance.

"What's the matter?" Bess asked.

"Look! There's Fingers Malone!"

6

A Spooky Search

It almost seemed as if the crook could feel the intent stares Nancy and Bess were aiming at him. Malone's gaze swept back and forth; he was evidently keeping a sharp lookout for park policemen and likely victims whose pockets he might pick. As his glance took in the two girls, his eyes lingered on Nancy Drew.

A startled, angry look came over the man's face. It was obvious that he had just recognized the teenage sleuth who had caused him and his partners so much trouble yesterday afternoon. The next instant, he took to his heels!

Nancy went after him on the run, her friend following close behind.

"Oh, dear! What'll happen if we catch up with him?" Bess worried aloud.

"Let's hope we sight Officer Doyle or that detective from St. Louis," Nancy shot back. "We'll try to draw their attention!"

"What if we don't?"

"We'll think of something!"

Bess moaned anxiously, "Please remember what they both told you about those two crooks, Nancy—they're dangerous!"

From the way Bess was panting, Nancy could tell that her plump friend was getting winded. By now, she could also see that Fingers Malone was heading for the Haunted House.

Out of the corner of her eye, Nancy glimpsed a girl waving at her from a distance, but she was too intent on watching Fingers to find out who the girl was or what she wanted.

Evidently, the crook had purchased a roll of general tickets on sale at the park entrance, good for all rides and concessions. Instead of lining up now to pay his admission, he simply tore off the required number, shoved them at the ticket taker, and darted past him into the Haunted House.

Nancy hastily debated the best course of action, then blurted at Bess, "Keep watch outside the exit. If you see a policeman, signal him. If

Fingers comes out, keep him in sight."

"Okay, but what about you?"

"I'm not sure myself—I'll just have to play it by ear, I guess."

Nancy fretted at the delay, but rather than cause any resentment or disturbance, she waited in line to pay her admission. Then she identified herself to the ticket taker and said, "A wanted criminal just went in the house a few minutes ago. Please find a policeman and tell him I've spotted Fingers Malone. I'll try to locate him inside!"

The ticket taker nodded tensely. "Sure thing. You watch yourself now, Miss Drew!"

Nancy hurried on into the Haunted House. Its interior was gloomy and ill-lit. Spiderwebs festooned the ceiling and corners, and weird, evil-looking portraits hung on the damp-stained walls.

Mournful organ music drifted down from somewhere on the upper floors. The excited voices and jittery laughter of other visitors who had entered the house just before her could be heard from adjoining rooms.

Nancy wondered which way to turn. Had she been foolish to follow Fingers Malone into the Haunted House? But no, she decided firmly—it was essential to find him and keep him under surveillance until the police could arrive to arrest him.

A curving staircase led up to the second floor. She could glimpse white, ghostly shapes flitting through the darkness above the landing. A beady-eyed rat, perched on one of the steps, seemed to be watching her intently. Nancy assumed the repulsive little creature was stuffed, but preferred not to check.

Anyhow, she felt it was unlikely that Malone would go upstairs, where he might be more easily trapped and have fewer possible escape routes.

Instead, she turned off into a corridor on her right. At the end of it was a closed doorway. Someone began thumping on the door from the other side, shouting, *"Let me out! . . . Let me out!"*

Nancy's heart beat faster. Was this another Haunted House trick, or was it possible that Malone had robbed someone after entering and had locked up his victim?

Taking a deep breath, Nancy reached out to unlock the door—then jumped back with a start as a grinning skeleton popped out at her with a bloodcurdling scream!

As her foot touched the moth-eaten carpet behind her, the floor seemed to give way under her weight. The next thing Nancy knew, she was plunging down a chute into utter darkness!

She landed on what felt like a swarming mass of small, furry objects. With a little cry of fright, Nancy scrambled away from them. A faint, moaning voice, accompanied by the sound of a clanking chain, reached her ears. Nancy groped her way toward it.

As her eyes became more used to the darkness, she saw that she was in a dusty, cobwebbed cellar. Ghoulish figures with glowing eyes could be glimpsed lurking furtively behind huge wine casks and amid the broken furniture and other discarded trash that littered the area.

Shuddery black batwings fluttered past—mostly overhead, but now and then one brushed her face. Nancy gulped hard, but did her best not to let her nerves get away from her. After all, it's just carnival trickery! she kept reminding herself.

The moaning voice and clanking chain sounded louder now. On her left, Nancy saw a faint glow of light. As she moved toward it, a wizened, sharp-featured face suddenly came into view.

It was that of Fingers Malone!

Nancy gasped with excitment, and almost in the same instant, Malone turned and fled!

Picking up the first makeshift weapon she could lay a hand on, which happened to be a broken chair leg, Nancy ventured cautiously in pursuit.

The stone walls of the cellar seemed to merge closer together at this point to form a winding, upward-sloping tunnel. As Nancy entered it, she thought she could hear faint footsteps in the distance.

Rounding a corner, she caught a fleeting glimpse of Fingers Malone darting up a flight of stone steps at the end of the tunnel!

Nancy quickened her pace. Just then came a deafening sound! It was only an artificial thunderclap that was part of the Haunted House sound tape, Nancy assumed when her heart sank back into place from out of her throat again. But for all that, the unexpected *ka-boom!* had left her pulse racing!

An eerie wind and the splatter of a storm added to the spooky ambience. Clutching the broken chair leg tighter for security, Nancy began tiptoeing up the stone steps.

At the top was an open doorway, through which the glow of light was coming. Nancy plunged through the opening at a rush, to dodge any sneak attack by Fingers Malone.

But she failed to move fast enough! As she

dashed through the doorway, a lightning blow caught Nancy on the back of the head, and darkness engulfed her!

When she finally came to, she seemed to be lying on an old, black horsehair sofa, and faces were hovering over her. Gradually she realized that she was in the front parlor of the Haunted House. But now the room was brightly illuminated, and the faces bending over her were those of Officer Doyle, the St. Louis detective, and the park nurse.

"Just lie quietly for a while, dear," the nurse said. "How do you feel?"

"I—I'm all right now, thank you," Nancy said and rose slowly to a sitting position. She winced slightly and fingered a sore spot on her scalp.

"Can you remember what happened?"

"Yes, someone hit me on the back of the head." Nancy halfway expected to feel a goose-egg there, but her thick, wavy, red-gold hair had evidently helped to protect her from injury.

Turning to the two policemen, she added, "I saw Fingers Malone, but he hid behind a door and took me by surprise."

"Are you sure?" asked Officer Doyle. From his doubtful expression, and a similar look on the face of Detective Norris, Nancy saw that they were not convinced.

"Well, of course I'm sure," she retorted. "I certainly saw him well enough yesterday to know what he looks like. Why?"

"Because we ordered both the entrance and exit doors locked as soon as we got here," Doyle replied, "and then we checked every person who was inside, one by one."

"Fingers Malone wasn't among them," Norris added. "And he's not in the house, either. We searched the place before you came to."

"But I saw him," Nancy insisted. She told the two officers exactly what had happened inside the Haunted House, and ended, "If you didn't see Malone, then he must have gotten away before you arrived."

Officer Doyle frowned. "That doesn't seem too likely, Nancy. He wouldn't have had time."

She pondered for a moment, then brightened. "Wait, I know how we can find out for sure!"

"How?"

"My friend Bess was waiting outside the exit. I told her to keep watch for Malone and follow him if he came out!"

Doyle glanced at his colleague, who shrugged. "It's worth a shot. Let's go and see what she says."

Nancy's blond friend was still standing outside the Haunted House, among the onlookers who had gathered after the arrival of the police.

"Oh, Nancy! Thank goodness you're all right!" Bess exclaimed and gave her a hug of relief. "I was so worried!"

"Never mind," Nancy assured her with a smile. "As you see, I'm okay. But what about Fingers Malone? Didn't you follow him?"

Bess looked puzzled. "Well, of couse not. He never came out. Isn't he under arrest?"

7

A Redheaded Visitor

"No, we haven't arrested Malone," Officer Doyle told Bess. "We can't find him. He's not in the house, and you say he never came out."

"No, I'm sure he didn't," Bess declared. "I've been keeping watch on the exit ever since we got here. . . ." Her voice trailed off into silence and she stared in bewilderment, first at the two policemen and then at Nancy.

The latter was both puzzled and embarrassed. She was sure the man she had chased was Fingers Malone. Bess had seen him, too. The way he had fled more or less proved they had made no mistake in recognizing the pickpocket.

Yet now he seemed to have vanished into thin air! What made it all the more frustrating and annoying was the way Officer Doyle and Detective Norris were looking at her. Obviously, they both put her story down to an overactive imagination.

"If I didn't see Fingers Malone, who hit me on the head?" she demanded.

An uncomfortable expression came over Norris's face, and he cleared his throat before replying. "Well, Miss Drew, in your excitement you probably ran into something."

"Then I must have been running backward, to get hit on the back of my head—is that what you're saying?"

The detective shrugged sheepishly. "Maybe you turned to glance over your shoulder and bumped into the door frame, who knows?"

"Don't worry about it, girls," Officer Doyle spoke up. "We'll nab Malone sooner or later if he's anywhere in the park."

And with that, the two policemen walked off. Nancy and Bess exchanged rueful looks and started back to the marina parking lot where the teenage sleuth had left the car.

"Gee, I just don't understand where that crook went, do you, Nancy?" Bess said.

"No, but I intend to find out before this case is over. We can discuss that later, though—right now I'm too hungry."

Bess giggled. "Stop stealing my lines!"

Laughing and chatting, the two girls drove back to the Drews' house and found George Fayne waiting there for them.

"Oh, great!" Nancy exclaimed happily. "Let's get some lunch."

"There's a big bowl of salad in the refrigerator and some sliced cold chicken," Hannah Gruen told her after greeting the two. "Would you like me to make some sandwiches?"

"We'll do it, Hannah," Nancy smiled.

"By the way, you've had more phone calls about the carousel mystery," the housekeeper reported and added with a wry chuckle, "My, oh my, you wouldn't believe what crazy ideas people have! One man asked me to tell you that a dray horse died from heatstroke, years ago, in the street just outside the park. He thinks its ghost may be turning the merry-go-round at night."

In response to the girls' queries, Hannah Gruen described several other far-out theories suggested by Nancy's phone callers. The three friends discussed them as they nibbled their sandwiches and salad on the big, cheerful sun porch.

"Maybe there's a park poltergeist," said George only half seriously.

"Isn't that the kind of ghost that throws things

around in haunted houses?" Bess asked her cousin.

"Right—usually when there's a scatter-brained teenager somewhere on the premises. And remember," George teased, "*you* often go to Riverside Park."

Bess responded by playfully throwing a piece of carrot at her. When the laughter subsided, Nancy said, "Anyhow, I'm not ready to accept any ghost theories—*yet*. At least not until I've checked out all the possible natural causes. That's why I intend to have an engineer examine the carousel—to see if it's been tampered with."

"Any particular engineer in mind?" George asked.

Nancy shook her head. "No, can you suggest someone?"

"Oh, I know!" Bess exclaimed, smiling.

George frowned at her cousin. "Bess, don't be childish!" Turning to Nancy, she said, "As a matter of fact, I have a friend who's studying electrical engineering in college. You haven't met him yet, but his name's Neil Sawyer."

"Is he here in River Heights?"

"Yes, he has a summer job at a recording studio on Maple Street."

"Sounds just right for the job!" Nancy smiled

happily. "Do you think he'd do it?"

"Oh, he'd be delighted to—if George asked him!" It was Bess's turn to tease, and she was rewarded by seeing her cousin blush.

As Nancy got up to serve the lemon chiffon pie, she mused aloud, "Just for the sake of argument, let's say some human joker is making the carousel act up at night. What possible reason could anyone have for playing such a trick?"

"Maybe someone doesn't like the owner, so he's trying to scare away customers," put in George.

Nancy nodded thoughtfully. "Clever idea . . . only if that's his game, it doesn't seem to be working very well. It would make a better publicity gimmick, wouldn't it, to *attract* business?"

"Guess you're right," George agreed. "There were certainly a lot of riders when we were at the park with the Custer kids."

"Mm, this is delicious!" Bess said, taking a forkful of pie. "You know, I saw a movie about a bank robbery on TV the other night. In the film, the thieves purposely started a fire in another building to distract the cops' attention while they were looting the bank vault."

Nancy flashed a startled glance at her friend.

"You mean, someone may be using the carousel the same way—to draw the attention of any policemen in the park area, while a crime's being committed somewhere nearby?"

"Something like that," Bess said timidly. "I guess it's a pretty wild idea, huh?"

"Maybe and maybe not," returned Nancy. "I'd say it's worth following up."

When they had finished eating, the girls carried their lunch things into the kitchen and washed the dishes. In ten minutes, all was neat again.

"Nancy, don't forget about our cookout tonight," Bess said as the two cousins prepared to leave.

"No danger," Nancy said with an eager smile.

"Let me just run upstairs and tell Hannah. Then I'll drive you two home."

"Mind if I use your phone?" asked George.

"Help yourself."

By the time Nancy came downstairs again, George was just hanging up. "I just called Neil Sawyer. He says he'll check the carousel for you this afternoon."

"Oh, marvelous!"

After dropping Bess and George at the Faynes' house, Nancy drove on to police headquarters, where she asked to see her friend, Police Chief McGinnis.

"How goes the carousel mystery, Nancy?" the stocky, gray-haired officer inquired after offering her a chair facing his desk.

"At the moment, I'm still baffled, Chief," the young detective confessed.

"Any way I can help?"

"Actually, I was wondering if the police might have a record of the dates and times the carousel started playing by itself at night."

McGinnis nodded, "Yes, we've had calls from the public every time, so there should be a complete record in the precinct log. Like me to find out?"

"If you would, I'd certainly appreciate it," Nancy replied. "Also, I'd like to know whether any crimes were committed in the area around the park at those same times."

"Sure, no problem. I'll check it out and get back to you," the police chief promised.

After thanking him and chatting a while longer, Nancy left headquarters and drove home. As she walked into the house, Hannah stuck her head around the kitchen door.

"Nancy, you just missed a visitor."

"Oh, who?"

"A red-haired girl named Joy Trent. She phoned this morning. Remember my telling you about a girl who wanted you to solve a mystery for her?"

"Oh yes, I do remember, Hannah. What did you tell her?"

"I said you'd been so busy you hadn't had time to return all your calls yet, but you'd be in touch with her as soon as possible. She seemed like a very nice girl—very polite," the housekeeper added approvingly. "She even apologized for bothering me, and said she hoped she wasn't making a nuisance of herself."

"I'll call her right now," Nancy decided.

"Oh no, you won't be able to reach her, I'm afraid. She said she'd be out most of the afternoon and evening," Hannah explained, "but if you could call her sometime tomorrow, she'd appreciate it."

Fleetingly, Nancy was reminded of something, but couldn't quite call it to mind. "What did this Joy Trent look like, Hannah?"

"Oh, I'd say she was a bit younger than you, Nancy, and she had very coppery red hair and freckles. Also, I imagine her parents must be very well-to-do, because her clothes were lovely and she was driving a very expensive-looking, foreign sports car."

61

Nancy knit her brow thoughtfully, but finally shook her head. "I feel I should know her from somewhere, Hannah, but I can't place her."

"I think you'd have a hard time forgetting this girl, dear," said the housekeeper. "Not only does she have red hair and freckles, but when I was talking to her, I noticed her eyes were two different colors. One was green and one brown."

Nancy gave up, despite a recollection that was flickering on the edge of her memory. "Guess I'll have to wait till I see her."

She spent the rest of the afternoon returning telephone calls that Hannah had noted down or that had been recorded on the answering machine. Late in the day, Nancy showered and changed into blue jeans and a pale blue knit pullover top, since George had said not to dress up.

Calling out to Hannah, "I'm leaving for George and Bess's cookout now!" Nancy went out to her blue sports car and drove to the Faynes' house. A number of cars were parked in front. Nancy recognized several as belonging to friends of the two cousins.

As she walked around to the backyard of the pleasant, old colonial house, the sound of laughter and chatter reached her ears. A number of people, young and old, were sitting or standing around. The barbecue fires had been lit and buffet tables of food set out.

With whoops of delight, the three Custer children cornered Nancy. "I've told my mom all about you," said Janet, "and now I want you to come and meet her!"

Nancy was propelled by the youngsters toward a pleasant-faced, curly-haired woman who was chatting with Mrs. Marvin and Mrs. Fayne. But she had only a few minutes to get acquainted with Mrs. Custer before George and a blond young man in horn-rimmed glasses came over to join them.

"Nancy, I want you to meet Neil Sawyer," said George. "He's already checked out the carousel! Isn't that great?"

"Wonderful!" Nancy smiled at George's new friend. "I'm happy to meet you, Neil—and I really appreciate your taking the trouble to inspect the carousel so promptly. Did you find anything of interest?"

"I sure did," Neil grinned back. "In fact, I believe I can tell you how the trick is done!"

8

Radio Gimmick

Nancy's eyes sparkled with interest. "Can you explain it to someone who knows nothing about electrical engineering?"

Neil nodded. "Sure, there's nothing very complicated about it. Do you know what a radio relay is?"

"Not really." Nancy dimpled and shook her head.

"Okay, well think of it as a kind of switch that turns something on and off. Only you don't have to push it with your finger, as you would a light switch."

"Why not?"

"Because it's a *remote-control* switch that's operated by a radio signal."

"You mean, a person could be some distance from the carousel and start it or stop it that way?"

"Exactly. All he'd need is a radio transmitter to beep out a signal of the right frequency."

"How far away would he have to be?" Nancy inquired keenly.

Neil Sawyer shrugged. "Anywhere from a few feet to a few miles, or even farther, depending on how powerful a transmitter he used."

"And how big would the radio relay be?"

"Very small. If it was attached to a magnet, it could be clamped underneath the operator's control box, and you'd never even notice it."

Neil said that old-fashioned carousels, dating back before the turn of the century, worked by steam power, which was also used to pump the band organ that played the merry-go-round music. But nowadays carousels are run by electric motors, and the music comes from an electronic tape.

"The radio relay," he went on, "would have two little wires with alligator clips on the end, so they could snap onto the wires coming out of the operator's control box."

"In other words," Nancy said, "whoever played the trick would just have to stick the relay in place underneath the control box, and then clip on the two wires?"

"Right. Even a kid could do it in seconds. And to remove it, he'd just unsnap the wires and pull off the relay."

Teenagers and adults occasionally rode the merry-go-round. Neil guessed that the prankster could deftly attach such a device without being noticed, while customers were getting on and off the carousel between rides. And it could be removed just as easily the next day—or, for that matter, during the night after the carousel had performed its spooky routine.

"Is there any sort of clue that might tell us whether or not a radio relay was used the way you described?" Nancy asked thoughtfully.

"Yes, though I wouldn't call it proof," Neil replied. "Some of the insulated covering is worn away from the wires that come out of the control box. And I noticed several scratch marks that *might* have been made by alligator clips."

Nancy thanked the engineering student for his help. Neil's theory gave her the exciting hope that she might now be one step closer to a solution of the haunted carousel mystery.

Next morning after breakfast, she called the red-haired girl who had come to the house. The phone was answered by a sharp-voiced woman.

"May I speak to Joy Trent, please?" Nancy said politely.

"Joy's not here. Who's calling?" was the curt

response. Somehow, the woman managed to sound bossy, impatient, and inquisitive, all at the same time.

"My name is Nancy Drew. Joy left a message asking me to get in touch with her."

"Hmph, what was your name again?"

"Nancy Drew."

"All right, I'll tell her you called," the woman said grudgingly and hung up.

Nancy put down the phone with a wry smile. Whoever the woman was, her telephone manner was anything but gracious.

Nancy was about to turn away into the living room when the phone rang. She picked up the receiver again. Her caller was Ned Nickerson.

"I'm back from Emerson," he reported. "How about lunch?"

"Sounds wonderful!" Nancy replied, her spirits instantly rising. "Where should we meet?"

"You name it."

"Well, let me see. I have to go to Riverside Park again. . ."

"Say no more, I'll meet you there. Eleven-thirty be okay?"

"Perfect!"

After hanging up, Nancy told Hannah Gruen her plans for the day. Later that morning, she found a space for her blue sports car in the parking lot adjoining the amusement-ride area, and strolled across the park toward the carousel.

As she approached it, she saw a woman talking to the merry-go-round owner, Leo Novak. The woman, about 40, was attractive and well dressed. She was showing Novak a piece of paper that looked like a newspaper or magazine clipping. As she spoke, she gestured toward the carousel. Novak shrugged and shook his head in response.

Nancy paused, not wanting to intrude on the conversation. The woman took a card and pen from her purse. She wrote something on the card, handed it to Novak, then turned away.

Nancy resumed her approach. By the time she was able to speak to Leo Novak, the woman was some distance away.

"Do you mind telling me who that lady was?" Nancy asked the ride owner.

"Aw, just some busybody who's read all that hokum in the news about my haunted merry-go-round," Novak brushed off her query.

Nancy noticed that he was wearing a large eye patch. "By the way, what's wrong with your eye?" she inquired sympathetically. "Nothing serious, I hope?"

The owner seemed embarrassed by her question. "Got a speck in it last night, that's all. This morning, it was still sore. It'll clear up."

"Perhaps you should see a doctor, Mr. Novak," Nancy advised. Then she told him Neil Sawyer's theory of how the carousel might have been turned on and off by a radio-relay device.

Leo Novak, however, scoffed at the idea. "No way!" he retorted. "You can take it from me, if any gimmick like that had been planted under the control box, I'd have noticed it."

Nancy was not convinced, but didn't wish to take time to argue. She was eager to find and interview the woman she had seen talking to the carousel operator. Nancy was intrigued by the way she had written something on a card and handed it to Novak, as if asking him to get in touch with her later.

But why would she do that, Nancy wondered, unless her interest in the merry-go-round was more serious or more important than Mr. Novak cared to admit?

As she turned away, Nancy caught a fleeting glimpse of the skin under the edge of his eye patch. It seemed dark and swollen. Gee, I wonder if he's got a black eye? she thought. If so, that might explain his look of embarrassment when she inquired why he was wearing the patch.

Nancy hurried off, shading her eyes to scan the throng of people milling about the park. But the mystery woman was no longer in sight. After searching the amusement park for a while, she gave up with a sigh and glanced at her wristwatch. It was almost 11:30. Uh-oh, Ned may be waiting for me! Nancy reminded herself.

Sure enough, Ned was in the parking lot. He waved as she approached and got out of his car to greet her with a kiss.

"How about the Limehouse Tavern for lunch?"

Nancy smiled. "Fine with me! I'd love some fish and chips."

The tavern, not far from Riverside Park, was run by an ex-London cockney and his wife. Nancy and Ned both loved its nautical atmosphere, reminiscent of an English dockside pub, and always found the food delicious.

As they ate, Nancy asked, "Did you get your fall program straightened out?"

"Yes, no problem. Which reminds me. Do you remember Professor Jenner?"

"Of course, you introduced me to him at the May Day Ball. Teaches art history, doesn't he?"

"That's the guy." Ned nodded. "He wants me to ask you a favor. Ever hear of an artist named Walter Kruse?"

"The Western painter and sculptor?"

"Right—in fact he started out as a cowboy, I hear. Anyhow, the prof's writing a book about Kruse . . . and he also caught a TV news report about you tackling the mystery of that haunted carousel."

Nancy was amused and slightly bewildered. "I'm not sure I see the connection," she said with a chuckle.

"There is one, believe it or not. It seems the news broadcast showed the carousel—including its name, the *Wonderland Gallop*. And according to Professor Jenner, Walter Kruse once had a girlfriend whose father owned that carousel."

Nancy was surprised and charmed by this bit of information. She remembered reading that the artist had passed away a year or two ago. From her impression of Kruse's age, she guessed that Professor Jenner must be referring to the *Wonderland Gallop*'s original owner—the man whom Leo Novak had once worked for.

Ned related that the romance had occurred during a brief period when Walter Kruse was employed as an amusement-park roustabout. Soon afterward, the artist had gone to New York and his work became famous; but for a while he had kept up a correspondence with the carousel owner's daughter in which he expressed his thoughts about painting and sculpture.

"That's what Kruse once told the prof, anyhow," Ned concluded. "So now that he's writing a book about him, Professor Jenner would like to see those letters, if the owner's daughter still has them. And he's hoping you can help him get in touch with her."

"I'll be glad to try," Nancy promised. Since Ned had to work that afternoon, he drove Nancy back to Riverside Park, where she had left her car.

I may as well ask Mr. Novak right now about the owner's daughter, Nancy reflected. So she strolled through the parking lot toward the amusement-ride area.

"Oh, Miss Drew!" called a youthful voice.

Nancy turned and saw a pretty teenage girl with flaming red hair waving at her. The girl was hastily getting out of a sleek, powerful-looking, foreign sports car.

Nancy guessed at once that she must be Joy Trent—and suddenly, she also realized why Hannah's description of the redheaded visitor had sounded familiar.

This was the girl who had waved to her yesterday when she was chasing Fingers Malone toward the Haunted House!

9

Nocturnal Break-In

The redheaded girl hurried over to Nancy's car and said, "I recognized you from your picture in the paper. I'm Joy Trent, Miss Drew. I must seem like an awful pest!"

"Not at all." Nancy smiled. "I'm happy to meet you. I understand you have a mystery you'd like me to help you solve."

Joy nodded. "It'll take awhile to tell you about it. Unfortunately, I have a meeting with our family lawyer in about fifteen minutes. Could you possibly come to lunch tomorrow at my house? We don't live too far from each other."

"Of course, Joy," Nancy assented. "That would be nice."

"Besides, we can talk a lot more comfortably there than we can in a parking lot. I live at 52 Sycamore Lane, by the way." With a grin and a wave of her hand, Joy went back to her car, then turned to call out, "Around twelve be all right?"

"Fine!" Nancy responded.

The red-haired girl slid behind the wheel and with a soft, throaty purr from her car's powerful engine drove out of the lot.

Nancy watched the sleek, foreign sports model admiringly. Then she walked into the amusement park, hoping to find Leo Novak on duty at his carousel.

As it turned out, she was in luck. The glum-faced concessionaire looked none too happy to see Nancy. But when he found out she had come to ask him about the former owner's daughter, his manner loosened up and he talked willingly.

"Sure, I remember Nina Ogden. Real pretty girl. She and I were about the same age," he said nostalgically. "Wouldn't have minded going out with her myself, but old man Ogden never paid me enough in those days to show her a real good time. Anyhow"—Novak's lips tightened—"she kind of looked down on me."

The name of the artist, Walter Kruse, however, rang no bells in his mind. "I dunno anything about him or any letters he wrote her. All I know is, she got married to some guy she met in college and moved away. Last time I saw her was when Mr. Ogden died. She inherited the *Wonderland Gallop*, so I bought it from her."

"Do you happen to remember her married name, or where she was living then?"

Novak frowned thoughtfully, then shrugged and shook his head. "'Fraid not . . . sorry."

Nancy was disappointed that she would not be able to provide Professor Jenner with any useful information. However, she felt that Nina Ogden's married name and last known address could probably be obtained from the official records of her father's death.

The next morning, shortly after breakfast, Nancy received a phone call from an upset Joy Trent. "Our house was broken into last night!" she reported.

"Oh dear, I'm sorry to hear that, Joy. Was anything taken?"

"We're not sure yet. My aunt's checking now. Nancy, could you come a bit earlier than we planned and look into this? Maybe you can help the police in some way."

"Of course, if I can," Nancy said soothingly. "Would eleven be all right?"

"Thanks, that would be great!" Joy sounded relieved as she hung up.

Nancy had just turned away from the telephone when it shrilled again. This time, her caller was Police Chief McGinnis.

"I've checked out that information for you, Nancy, about any trouble that occurred near the park at the same time the carousel played at night. There's only one case that fits, and that's the theft of a boat on the river—it happened just below the hill on which Riverside Park is located."

McGinnis added that the theft had occurred during the merry-go-round's last spooky outburst on Monday night, which was the same night that Nancy and Ned had kept watch.

"That's interesting, Chief," the girl sleuth replied. "I suppose the police have the name and address of the boat owner?"

"Sure, do you want that information?"

"Yes, please—it might be helpful."

"Well then, here it is. Do you have a pencil and paper handy?" When Nancy said yes, he dictated the information.

"One last thing, Chief. A friend of mine just told me her house was broken into last night— the Trents on Sycamore Lane. Do you have anything on that?"

"Hang on, Nancy—I'll see."

A few moments later, the police chief's hearty voice came back on the phone. "Well, well—this may interest you, Nancy! It seems we got an anonymous phone tip about that burglary. The dispatcher sent a police car to the scene, and apparently it interrupted the heist, but the crooks got away."

Nancy thanked Chief McGinnis and hung up thoughtfully. "That's odd," she said aloud. This was the second time in just a few days that the police had been tipped off about criminals who in some way were involved with her own sleuthing. First had come the phone tip on Tuesday, which Officer Doyle had mentioned, about Fingers Malone and Baldy Krebs being seen in Riverside Park. And now, last night, there was another, about the break-in at Joy Trent's house.

And both tips had proven correct!

Is there some connection, Nancy wondered, or is all this just a coincidence? The second call, of course, could have been phoned in by some neighbor or even a passerby who did not wish to become involved . . .

Just then, Nancy heard the clock in the living room begin to chime the hour. She glanced at her wristwatch. Goodness, if she was going to pick up Hannah's order from the market before going to Joy's house, she'd have to hurry!

Quickly changing into a pale yellow linen dress and a pair of white dress sandals, Nancy transferred her wallet, makeup, and keys to a slim, white shoulder bag and set off on her errand.

Sometime later, having dropped Hannah's order off at home and left her a note, Nancy was turning up the drive to the Trents' house. It loomed ahead, beyond the trees and shrubbery—a large, impressive-looking stone mansion with a red tile roof.

She had just come through an arching entrance gateway when a silver-colored, two-door sedan passed her on its way out. Nancy caught her breath and did a hasty double take. At the wheel of the other car was the same woman she had seen talking to Leo Novak at the amusement park yesterday!

Nancy parked in the drive, walked up the stone steps of the house, and rang the bell. A smiling, silver-haired butler in a black uniform answered the door promptly and ushered her into a spacious, wide-windowed room with comfortable chairs and a baby grand piano. "Miss Drew, madam."

A thin, middle-aged woman, with a disagreeable expression, rose from a delicate writing desk and waved Nancy to a chair. "I'm Joy's aunt. I expect her back very shortly."

"I hope your friend didn't cut short her visit on my account," Nancy probed. "I saw a woman driving off just as I arrived."

A flash of anger passed over her hostess's face. "She's no friend of mine—that troublesome busybody! As far as I'm concerned, she had no business coming here, and I've no wish to see her again!"

10

The Iris Riddle

Nancy was surprised by the furious way Joy's aunt responded to her remark, so she did not pursue the matter, even though she was still curious about the visitor's identity and why she had come to call on the Trents.

Luckily, the awkward silence that followed was soon broken as Joy's car was heard pulling into the drive. The red-haired teenager came bursting eagerly into the house, having seen Nancy's blue sports car parked outside.

"I'm so sorry to have kept you waiting, Nancy!" she apologized breathlessly. "I expected to be back long before you arrived, but I got a flat tire on the way home."

"It doesn't matter a bit, Joy." Nancy smiled.

"I've only been here a few minutes."

"You've met my Aunt Selma?"

"Well, yes—though I didn't catch her name."

"Mrs. Yawley," said Joy, performing a belated introduction. "Aunt Selma, this is Nancy Drew, the famous girl detective. I'm hoping she can help me figure out Daddy's last message."

The woman inclined her head and shook hands coldly. "I'm never sure it's wise to discuss family affairs with outsiders," she murmured with an air of disapproval. "I trust you know what you're doing, Joy."

Without giving either her niece or Nancy time to respond, Mrs. Yawley turned and left the room.

Joy sighed but managed to grin at Nancy. "Don't mind Aunt Selma. She's nicer than she seems. The only trouble is, she treats me like a little, backward child who can hardly be trusted to cross the street by herself."

Nancy wondered if this meant Mrs. Yawley was Joy's guardian, but refrained from asking. Instead, she changed the subject and brought up last night's break-in.

Joy related that the burglars had evidently entered the house through a basement window, but had stumbled in the dark while coming upstairs. The noise had awakened the butler, who slept on the ground floor. When he went to investigate, she said he was overpowered by two men in ski masks. One clamped a hand over the butler's mouth to prevent any outcry while he was being tied and gagged.

"After that, he could hear them moving around in different parts of the house," Joy went on, "but the police got here about ten minutes later. I guess the robbers must have heard the scout car pulling up outside. Anyhow, they both got away without being seen or caught."

"Do you know what was stolen?" Nancy asked.

"Nothing—that's the funny part of it!"

"You're quite sure?"

"Oh yes, Aunt Selma checked over every room."

"Hm, that is odd." Nancy frowned slightly. "Was anything out of place? Or was there any sign of ransacking—I mean, like drawers or cabinets being opened?"

Joy shook her head. "Not that any of us noticed. Why?"

"I just wondered if they might have been searching for valuables—you know, like taking inventory first, deciding what to steal—but they got interrupted by the police before they could scoop up the loot."

"Oh yes, I see what you mean. But there was

no sign of that. In fact, there were valuables in plain sight—like those silver candlesticks on the mantel—that they didn't even bother with."

"Have you any idea who called the police?"

Joy shrugged. "Not really. I just assumed they were patrolling the neighborhood and noticed something suspicious."

"No, they responded to a phone tip," Nancy said. "I have that from the police chief."

Joy was surprised by this information and looked thoughtful. "You know, Nancy, this may not be important, but I have a hunch I was followed home yesterday after I met you at the park."

"You mean another car followed yours?"

"Yes, I kept seeing it in my rearview mirror, even though I made several turns."

"Did you notice the license number?"

"No, I didn't even think of that," Joy said regretfully. "It was a dark blue car, and there was a man at the wheel. He zoomed on past after I turned off into our drive, so I never even got a good look at him."

Joy Trent had been showing Nancy around the house while she told her about the break-in. But now the two girls settled themselves on a sofa in the sitting room to chat and get better acquainted.

Joy revealed that she was an only child, and

an orphan, as Nancy had guessed. Her father, John Trent, who sounded like a hard-driving business executive with little time to spare, had died several months ago. Yet, despite his busy schedule, he had evidently been devoted to his daughter and had lavished a good deal of attention on her.

Joy could not even remember her mother, who had died when Joy was a mere toddler. But the little girl had enjoyed a fond, close relationship with her father. Otherwise, she had been brought up by a succession of housekeepers and governesses until recently, when Mr. Trent's sister—Joy's Aunt Selma—became widowed and moved in to live with them.

Nancy was still intrigued by the identity of the mystery woman, whom she had first seen at the park talking to Leo Novak, and then driving away from the Trents' house this morning. Could Joy's own visit to the park have had something to do with all this? Nancy wondered.

In view of Aunt Selma's harsh attitude toward the woman, she decided it might be better to probe for information in a roundabout fashion, rather than ask a blunt question.

"By the way," Nancy remarked, "I'm sorry I didn't respond when you waved to me at the park the other day."

"I'm surprised you even noticed me." Joy

grinned. "You seemed in quite a hurry."

"That's one way of putting it," Nancy said with a chuckle. "Actually, I was chasing a crook." She told the other girl about her adventure with the pickpockets and then asked casually, "Do you often go to the amusement park?"

"Not really, though I did when I was little." A reminiscent smile came over Joy's face as she went on, "I loved to ride the carousel! Daddy took me there whenever he could. In fact he even bought me my favorite steed on the merry-go-round."

"Really?" Nancy was startled; her sleuthing antennae instantly shot up. "How did that happen?"

"Well, at one time, the carousel moved away from River Heights."

"Yes, I know."

"There was one particular horse on it that I always used to ride," Joy explained. "It was the lead horse—the most beautiful creature you ever saw! When I found out the merry-go-round was about to be taken away, I was brokenhearted. So Daddy made a deal to buy the horse from the carousel owner and wrote him out a check then and there!"

Nancy's blue eyes twinkled. "You must have been a very pleased little girl!"

Joy laughed merrily. "Oh, you've no idea! It happened that the next day was my birthday. Daddy ordered a van to come and pick up the horse in time for my party, and my birthday celebration started right there at the park. It was quite an occasion!"

"I can imagine." *So this*, Nancy reflected, *was why the lead horse had to be replaced!* Why had Leo Novak told her a different story?

Aloud, she asked, "Do you still have the horse?"

"Oh, yes! I'm too fond of it to ever give it away, though right now it's at the River Heights Day-Care Center. I lent it so the children who stay there while their parents are working can have the fun of riding it."

Joy told Nancy that before her father became head of his own machine-tool company, he had started out as a lathe hand in a machine shop and was an expert handyman and machinist. "He mounted my horse on a special hobby-horse stand that he made himself, so it would jog up and down when I rode it. The stand even has a music box inside that winds up and plays when the horse gallops!"

"Sounds wonderful!" Nancy said, dimpling. "I'd love to see it."

"I'll take you to the day-care center some

time and show it to you," Joy promised. "Anyhow, it wasn't until I heard about the haunted
carousel on the TV news that I realized the
Wonderland Gallop was back in Riverside
Park—so naturally I had to go see it again. And
then, of course, I read in the paper how you had
agreed to try to solve the mystery—which is
what gave me the idea of asking you to solve
one for me."

"You've got me terribly curious," said Nancy.
"Tell me about *your* mystery."

"Maybe 'riddle' would be a better word for
it," Joy began slowly.

Before she could go any further, the butler
announced lunch. So Joy continued her story at
the table. "Just before my father died," she related with a slight catch in her voice, "he told
me he'd left something for me in the lower
right-hand drawer of his desk in the study. This
is what I found."

She handed Nancy an envelope addressed to
My darling daughter Joy. "Open it."

Nancy did so. Inside was a slip of paper bearing an odd message:

Iris = ? = Old Glory

"How strange!" Nancy murmured. "Do you

have any clue at all as to what it may mean?"

As Joy nodded in response, Nancy saw her eyes mist over. "Iris was my mother's name."

Nancy hesitated a moment. "Do you have any recollection of her?"

"None at all," Joy said sadly. "I don't even know what she looked like. Daddy didn't even have a snapshot to remember her by—and he always regretted it."

"Hmph!" Mrs. Yawley, who was lunching with them, had been glowering at the two girls ever since they began their conversation. Now she uttered an audible sniff of disapproval. "Is it really necessary to discuss all this with a stranger, Joy?"

The teenage redhead gave her a calmly defiant look. "I invited Nancy here to help me find out what Daddy's letter means, Aunt Selma. I can hardly expect her to do that, can I, without her knowing a few facts about my family."

The thin-lipped woman sniffed again and frowned irately, but remained silent for the rest of the meal.

Joy told Nancy that her parents had been young and poor when they got married; her mother, unhappily, had not lived long enough to enjoy John Trent's eventual success. Partly because he had no picture of his wife, Mr. Trent had surrounded himself with irises in various forms.

"For instance, if you'll notice," Joy went on, "this room has iris-patterned wallpaper. After lunch, I'll show you some other examples."

When they rose from the table, she led Nancy through several rooms, ending up in her father's study. In every room, there was at least one bowl or vase filled with irises. There were also ceramic and glass likenesses of the flower, wall paintings of irises, iris-decorated drapes, and numerous other such objects or furnishings.

"Your father must have cherished your mother's memory a great deal," Nancy murmured.

"Yes." Joy nodded and was silent for a moment, then went on. "Yet because of his grief, Daddy could never bear to talk about her much. So I really know very little about her."

"I suspect one of these examples of the iris motif may hold the answer to that cryptic message he left you," Nancy mused aloud. But for the moment, she was at a loss to unravel the puzzle—even though, privately, she had a feeling at the back of her mind that she had already sighted a clue somewhere in the house. So she asked Joy for time to think over what she had just learned, and promised to resume their conversation later.

After leaving the Trents' house, Nancy returned to the amusement park. She wanted to ask Leo Novak why he had told her the lead horse was replaced because of breakage, when actually the original had been sold to Joy Trent's father.

"Aw, that was way back when the Trent girl was just a little kid," he retorted impatiently. "It happened when Mr. Ogden owned the carousel—and the trailer. If you don't believe me, her dad had a photograph taken at the time and gave Ogden a copy—it's still stuck up on the wall of the trailer. I thought you wanted to know about the last time the lead horse was replaced. The truck accident I told you about happened after I took over the carousel."

"I see," Nancy said politely. "Well, thank you for explaining that to me, Mr. Novak."

Her next call was on the owner of the boat that had been stolen on the night she and Ned kept watch on the carousel.

The owner, a gas station operator named Vic Marsh, told her he had been fishing on the river that night, just below the park, when suddenly he saw the carousel light up and start playing music.

"Startled me out of my wits!" Marsh added with a chuckle. "So I went ashore and climbed up the hillside to see what was going on. Later on, when I came down again, I saw those two guys making off with my boat. It was too dark to see what they looked like, but I yelled and went after them. It was two against one, so I got roughed up a bit. They knocked me down and shoved off before I could stop them!"

Nancy's eyes widened as a thought struck her. The boat thieves could have been the two dark figures whom she and Ned had seen examining the carousel!

11

Romany Rendezvous

The more Nancy considered the question, the more certain she felt that the boat thieves were, indeed, the midnight intruders in the park. Rather than run out into one of the lighted streets that bordered Riverside Park on three sides—and thus run the risk of being spotted and captured—they had cleverly made their getaway in the darkness via the river, in the stolen boat.

"Did you ever get your boat back?" Nancy asked Vic Marsh.

"Oh yes, it was found abandoned the next morning, just a little ways downriver."

"And where is it now, Mr. Marsh?"

"Back on its trailer, in my driveway at home."

"How was it returned to you?" she inquired.

The gas station operator looked puzzled. "I went and picked it up myself, after the cops called me. Why?"

"Because if no one else handled it in between times, it may still have the thieves' fingerprints on it."

Vic Marsh's eyes lit up. "Hey, that's a smart idea!"

"Any objection if I ask the police to go to your house and check the boat?"

"Be my guest!"

Nancy called Police Chief McGinnis from a booth just outside the service station and explained her notion.

"Right you are, Nancy. I'll send one of our experts out to dust for prints this afternoon." The chief sounded enthusiastic. "I'll let you know the results."

Nancy drove directly home, hoping for a quiet hour or two in which to catch up on some chores. As she entered the house, the telephone was ringing.

When she answered, a pleasant woman's voice asked to speak to Nancy Drew.

"This is Nancy Drew," the girl replied.

"Miss Drew, you don't know me, but I'm the woman in the silver car whom you saw driving away from the Trent house this morning."

93

Nancy felt a thrill of excitement, but struggled to keep her own voice calm and casual. "Oh yes, I remember. But how did you know who I was, or where to reach me?"

"Because I recognized you from your picture in the newspaper story about the haunted carousel."

"I see. May I ask who's calling?"

There was a moment's hesitation at the other end of the line. "I'd rather not answer that question for the moment, Miss Drew, if you don't mind. It happens that I need your help. I wonder if I could meet with you somewhere."

Nancy was only too eager to learn more about her mysterious caller. "When did you have in mind?" she asked.

"Right away—or as soon as you possibly can," the woman answered in an urgent voice.

"Very well. Would you like to come here?"

"Oh—thanks but no, I'd prefer someplace else. If you could meet me at the Romany Tearoom in ten or fiften minutes, I'd appreciate it."

"Okay, I'll be there," Nancy promised and hung up.

The tearoom was located among a busy stretch of small shops on the fringe of downtown River Heights. After parking her car, she entered and saw the woman caller waving to her from a small, candle-lit table by the big, beige-curtained window.

"It was very good of you to come, Miss Drew." The woman smiled and, with a gesture of her hand, invited her guest to have a chair.

"I must confess, your call has made me very curious," said Nancy, sitting down.

"Small wonder! I apologize for being so mysterious, but as I said on the phone, there's a reason. May I assume you're a friend of Joy Trent?"

"Yes, I am," Nancy answered.

"Then I'd like to ask you a favor." The woman indicated a white cardboard box bearing a florist's label that was lying alongside her purse on the table. "Would you deliver this to Joy this afternoon?"

Nancy hesitated, troubled. She didn't know this woman, and no matter how nice she seemed outwardly, she might still mean harm to Joy.

"I don't mean to sound impolite or unfriendly," she murmured aloud, "but may I ask what's inside?"

The woman smiled. "You're quite right to be cautious, Miss Drew—I don't blame you a bit." Then she lifted the cover just enough to show that opening it entailed no danger. "But if you'd like to be absolutely sure, you can go and check with the florist."

She indicated the name on the box and then pointed out the tearoom window. "His shop is just across the street."

Nancy's slight, cautious frown relaxed into a sudden smile. She had decided to trust her own judgment of the woman's character. "Very well."

"Oh, thank you, Miss Drew! My name and phone number are inside the box. Would you be kind enough to call me and let me know the outcome of the delivery?"

As Nancy said yes, a waitress came to their table, carrying a tray of tiny, fancy sandwiches as well as cups, saucers, and a pot of steaming tea.

"I'm grateful to you for trusting me, Miss Drew." The woman's attractive face reflected Nancy's own smile. "Now let's have some tea!"

Fifteen minutes later, Nancy parted from her mysterious new acquaintance outside the Romany Tearoom. But instead of going straight to her car parked at the curb nearby, she stopped at an outdoor phone booth and called Joy Trent.

"Hi, Nancy!" the red-haired girl responded. "Don't tell me you've figured out my father's letter already?"

Nancy chuckled. "I'm afraid not, Joy. But something else has come up—something rather odd. I've been asked to deliver a package to you."

"To me?" Joy sounded surprised. "Who's it from?

"A woman who refuses to identify herself." The teenage sleuth briefly explained how the package had been entrusted to her.

"Oh gosh, now you've got me curious! Could you bring it right over?" Joy begged.

"I'm practically on my way!"

When Nancy arrived at the Trents' house, she found Mrs. Yawley on hand with Joy. Judging from her facial expression, the tight-lipped woman was as curious about the package as her niece.

Nancy debated briefly whether or not to mention that the woman she had met at the Romany Tearoom was the same person she had seen leaving the Trents' house earlier. But she judged it wiser not to bring this up for the time being. In any case, she had a strong hunch that Mrs. Yawley already suspected who had sent the package.

97

Joy took the florist box from Nancy and, with bated breath, untied it and removed the cover. A gasp escaped her lips, and her eyes brightened with excitement.

"Nancy! It's an *iris*!"

She held out the box long enough to show its contents. Inside lay a purple flower—and a folded note!

Joy hastily unfolded and read the message, then handed it to Nancy. It said:

> *If you care to get in touch with me, call the Regent Hotel and ask for Mrs. Rose Harrod in Room 922.*

"Here, let me see that!" said Mrs. Yawley, impolitely snatching the note away from Nancy.

"Golly," Joy blurted out, lifting the iris from the box, "this may mean she knows something about Mother—or about that letter Daddy left me! I'm going to call her right away!"

She started toward the phone, but stopped short as her aunt exclaimed harshly:

"Oh no, you're not! The woman who sent this is obviously nothing but a fraud and a troublemaker! Joy, I absolutely forbid you to contact that creature!"

12

Fog Curtain

Joy's eyes flashed rebelliously. "You've no right to take that attitude, Aunt Selma!" she protested.

"I've every right!" Mrs. Yawley snapped. "Just remember, young lady, I'm your legal guardian!"

"And maybe *you*'d better remember what Daddy's will said!" Joy's voice trembled with indignation.

The thin-lipped woman looked her niece up and down scathingly. "Just what are you referring to?"

"According to the lawyer, Mr. Trimble, his will only names you as my *temporary* guardian," Joy pointed out, holding up the iris. "So

99

don't think you can stop me forever from seeing the lady who sent this! You may not even remain my guardian until I'm twenty-one!"

If it's true that redheads have hot tempers, thought Nancy, Joy Trent certainly looks the part right at this moment! The young girl's cheeks were aflame behind their sprinkling of freckles, and her bright red hair added to her fiery look.

"Besides," Joy went on, "it's absurd to forbid me to see someone who may be able to tell me about my mother—or help to explain Daddy's riddle! What harm can it do, for goodness' sake, to hear whatever she has to say?"

Turning to her friend for support, Joy added, "Don't you agree, Nancy?"

Before the teenage sleuth could reply, Selma Yawley rounded on her, "You keep out of this, Miss Drew! You've caused enough trouble already by acting as that wretched woman's messenger!"

Nancy was not intimidated in the least by Mrs. Yawley's manner. Nevertheless, she thought it best not to take sides for the moment, even though there was no doubt where her own sympathies lay.

"Why not wait and ask me that question tomorrow, Joy?" she suggested with a calm smile.

"Perhaps you'll both see things in better perspective then. In the meantime, it's late, and I'd better be getting home."

It was hard to erase the unpleasant incident from her mind, however. At the dinner table that evening, she told her father what had happened and asked his opinion on the subject. "What should I have done, Daddy?"

"What did you *feel* like doing?" said Carson Drew, responding to her question with another question.

Nancy chuckled. "To be perfectly honest, I thought her aunt was behaving like a stuffy old witch, and I felt like telling Joy to use her own common sense and do just as she pleased. I mean, it seemed so unreasonable for Mrs. Yawley to forbid Joy even to speak to the woman!" Nancy's smile faded and she ended uncertainly, "The trouble was, I . . . well, I just wasn't sure I had any right to butt in."

"What about her father's point of view?"

"How do you mean?" inquired Nancy, raising an eyebrow.

"Presumably, this John Trent must have been a pretty shrewd judge of character to be so successful. Wouldn't he have had good reason for naming his sister to be Joy's guardian?"

"Perhaps he had no other choice—she may

101

have been the only other relative he had," said Nancy. "But, anyhow, that's just the point. According to Joy, the family lawyer, Mr. Trimble, said that her father's will only named Mrs. Yawley as Joy's *temporary* guardian. Also, that she might not continue as guardian until Joy was twenty-one. Doesn't that sound as if he wasn't wholly convinced Mrs. Yawley was the best choice?"

"Hm, you may have something there." Mr. Drew sipped his coffee thoughtfully for a moment. "And you say the lawyer's name is Trimble, eh? That would be Fred Trimble, I imagine. I've met him in court a few times and at the bar association dinners. Let me sound him out about this, Nancy, and see what he has to say."

"Oh Daddy, if you could, I'd be grateful!"

Nancy had just helped Hannah clear the table, when Bess and George arrived excitedly.

"Oh, Nancy, we're going to have a slumber party on the houseboat and we want you to come! Please say you will—it'll be fun!" Bess bubbled with enthusiasm and anticipation.

"Just the three of us, Nancy," George chimed in. "No babysitting tonight. The Custers are staying at my house tonight, and Uncle Bill said we could sleep on the boat if we wanted to . . . What do you say, Mr. Drew?" George appealed to a smiling Carson Drew.

"It certainly sounds attractive," he replied. "Sleeping on a river in good weather is very calming."

"I couldn't agree more, Dad." Nancy hugged him. "Come on, kids, and I'll throw some things in my overnight bag." Nancy turned and ran upstairs, her two friends trooping after her.

In her room, Nancy took a small zippered bag from her closet and folded her nightclothes into it. Then, with George and Bess's help, she collected comb, brush, and toiletries from her dressing table.

Minutes later, they had said good-bye to Carson Drew and Hannah Gruen, and were driving off to the marina in Nancy's little blue sports car.

The evening had turned sultry rather unexpectedly, and by the time they reached the houseboat, the moon had disappeared behind a bank of clouds.

"Gee, I hope it doesn't rain," Bess said plaintively.

"What's the difference? It'll just be more cozy." George laughed.

"Right," Nancy agreed. "Don't worry, Bess—we'll be safely docked at the marina."

Once aboard the houseboat, the girls changed into their nightclothes and made cocoa. Taking their cups out of the galley and going out on the small, open deck, the girls settled themselves in deck chairs and listened to the water gently lapping against the sides. At George's suggestion, they began telling each other ghost stories.

As a wispy fog drifted in from the river, the stories grew spookier and spookier. Finally, Bess called a halt. "If we don't stop right now, I won't be able to sleep for bad dreams! Let's go to bed."

Giggling, her friends agreed. Going back inside the cabin, they settled down in their bunk beds and, one by one, dropped off to sleep.

Sometime during the night, Nancy awoke . . . with an unpleasant sense of danger. What had awakened her?

With a sudden gasp of alarm, she realized that the houseboat was in motion! She could feel the deck swaying to and fro beneath her—far more than would have been the case if the boat were still safe in its sheltered slip at the marina.

It must have come loose from its moorings, Nancy realized. *We must be adrift on the river!*

Springing up from her bunk, she pulled on her robe and slippers and hurried out on deck. She shivered as the damp night air sent a chill through her body.

Thick layers of swirling mist surrounded the houseboat on all sides, and it was impossible to see more than a few yards in any direction. Yet despite the fog and darkness, there was no longer any doubt in Nancy's mind that the boat had come adrift.

If they were still in their berth, a faint, haloed glow should have been visible from the marina's dock lights. As it was, not even a glimmer pierced the dark, oily fog anywhere she looked!

The distant hoot of a foghorn and the muffled clang of a ship's bell reached her ears through the billowing mist. The eerie sounds racked Nancy with a thrill of apprehension.

Oh, what can we do?! she asked herself. The first thing, of course, was to wake Bess and George. Then they'd better start the engine and try to—

Nancy broke off with a sudden cry of fear and her eyes widened in fright.

The high, white bow of a good-sized motor cruiser had just loomed through the fog only a short distance away! *The craft was bearing straight down on them!*

13

Telltale Prints

For a moment, Nancy stood paralyzed with fear. Then she roused herself to action and began shouting, "*Stop!* . . . *Stop!*" at the top of her lungs.

She had no idea where to find the switch for the houseboat's running lights, but darting back inside, she at least turned on the cabin lights and also snatched up her handbag.

George and Bess had already been awakened by Nancy's loud cries. Bewildered, but realizing that some sort of emergency had arisen, they both jumped out of bed, wriggled into their robes, and followed her out on deck. The sight of the oncoming cruiser shocked them wide awake!

Nancy plucked a small flashlight from her bag and began shining its beam back and forth. The other two girls joined in her frantic shouts.

Just in the nick of time, the high, white prow of the cruiser veered away!

Presently, an angry male voice came bellowing through an electric bullhorn at the three trembling girls. *"What are you doing on the river without lights?!"*

As the other craft maneuvered into position alongside the houseboat, Nancy was able to explain that they had been securely moored at the River Heights marina, but that somehow the boat had come adrift during the night.

The cruiser skipper, by now sympathetic and concerned over the girls' plight, offered to tow them back to the marina if they would throw him their towline.

George hurried forward to haul it from the water under the cruiser's powerful searchlight. Nancy saw her gasp and frown when the end of the rope was in her hand.

"What's wrong, George?"

"See for yourself, Nancy!"

The end of the rope had been cleanly and freshly cut!

"We didn't just *come* adrift," George went on, putting their mutual thought into words. "Someone *cut* us loose from our mooring!"

Bess was nervous and shaken by this discovery, but Nancy tried to allay her fears. "Never mind, we can worry about that later," she soothed. "The most important thing right now is to get back to the marina!"

George tossed the line to the waiting cruiser captain, and he promptly took them in tow. Within an hour, the girls were back safe and sound in their slip at the marina. After thanking their rescuer emotionally, they lost no time in crawling back into their bunks, and all three were soon sinking into an exhausted slumber.

Next morning, the girls slept late. Then, after a light breakfast, Nancy dropped Bess and George at their homes and drove on to her own house.

"Nancy, your dad called about an hour ago," Hannah Gruen greeted her. "He's going to be in court the rest of the day, so he asked me to tell you that he's talked to Mr. Trimble, and you're to call him when you get in."

As she spoke, the housekeeper took Nancy's overnight bag and handed her a slip of paper bearing the lawyer's phone number.

"Okay, Hannah. Thanks." Nancy went to the front hall telephone and dialed the number.

When Hannah returned a few moments later,

she was just hanging up. "Well, I'm off to lunch with Mr. Trimble," the teenager reported. "It's the only time he can see me, so I'll just have time to change!"

Ten crowded minutes later, she was on her way to La Cuiller d'Argent, the restaurant where she had arranged to meet the attorney.

As she entered, Nancy was greeted by a dark-eyed headwaiter with a waxed mustache. "Mam'zelle Drew? M'sieu Trimble is waiting for you. Come this way, please."

He showed her to a table occupied by an elderly man with a mane of white hair.

"So you're Carson Drew's daughter!" The lawyer stood up with a smile and shook hands with the young sleuth.

"I'm very grateful to you for seeing me on such short notice." Nancy dimpled.

"Not at all, my dear. I don't often have a chance to lunch with a lovely young lady."

After they had ordered, Mr. Trimble said, "Now, how can I help you, Miss Drew?"

"I understand you were Mr. John Trent's lawyer. Could you tell me about him?" Nancy asked.

"Well, there's not much to tell, really. John Trent was a self-made man. He started from scratch, opened up his own small machine shop, and built it into a major machine-tool company. And made a fortune while doing so, I might add."

"Do you know much about his background or his past?"

"Not a great deal. I gathered from various remarks he made over the years that he came from a poor background—and he certainly adored his only child, Joy. A lovely girl, by the way."

Fred Trimble paused to offer Nancy a roll, then went on, "He never spoke about his wife, you see. Apparently, her death must have been a bitter blow. I do know that during most of the time I served as his personal attorney, he employed babysitters and housekeepers to care for Joy. And then, recently, his widowed sister, Selma Yawley, came to live with them to help out."

He fell silent while the white-coated waiter served their eggs Benedict. Once they were eating, Nancy said, "Joy mentioned something about her Aunt Selma being only her temporary guardian."

"Hmph." The lawyer cleared his throat, looking slightly uncomfortable. "Yes, well, my client was concerned that Joy might not be too happy under her aunt's guardianship. So he specified privately in his will that, under certain circumstances, other arrangements might be worked out."

"You mean, a different guardian might be appointed?"

"Ahem!" Once again Mr. Trimble looked uncomfortable. "I'm sorry, Miss Drew, but I'm not at liberty to discuss that subject. Joy is now seventeen. I can only tell you that when she reaches the age of twenty-one, she will come into her father's fortune. Until then, it will remain in trust under the control of myself, as the executor of his estate, and her guardian, who at present is Mrs. Yawley."

As she enjoyed her eggs Benedict, Nancy sat thinking of Mr. Trimble's phrase, "under certain circumstances." The question was, *what* circumstances?

Only one thing seemed clear, Nancy reflected. John Trent must have sensed instinctively that his sister, Selma Yawley, was not the ideal guardian for his beloved daughter, Joy!

The young detective and the elderly attorney finished their delicious meal while chatting pleasantly about various subjects.

"Thank you for a lovely lunch, Mr. Trimble," Nancy said as they parted.

"The pleasure was all mine, Miss Drew, I assure you!"

Nancy decided to call Joy Trent to arrange

another visit that afternoon. But on her way to the Trent house, she stopped off at police headquarters to speak to Chief McGinnis.

"Nancy! I was just going to phone you!" the chief declared as she walked into his office. "I just had a report from our fingerprint lab about that stolen boat."

"They found the prints of the boat thieves?" Nancy queried hopefully.

"That's right. And believe it or not, they belong to Fingers Malone and Baldy Krebs! Our boys matched them up with a complete set of prints Detective Norris brought us from the St. Louis Police Department."

"Oh, wow!" Nancy was excited. This news strongly suggested that Fingers and Baldy were the two dark figures whom she and Ned had seen on the carousel Monday night, and that they had made their getaway by stealing the boat, as she had already guessed.

But why were they so interested in the carousel?

After pondering for several moments, Nancy said, "Chief, is Detective Norris still in River Heights?"

"Yes, he's still keeping watch for those two crooks at Riverside Park."

"Is there any way I could reach him?"

"Sure, no problem." McGinnis promptly had a radio call sent out to the park policeman, Officer Doyle, asking him to have Detective Norris phone police headquarters.

Within a few minutes, the telephone rang on Chief McGinnis's desk. Detective Norris was on the line. After acknowledging the call, McGinnis handed the phone to Nancy.

"Nancy Drew here," she said. "I'd like to ask you a question, Detective Norris. You told me Fingers Malone was almost caught at the park in St. Louis, but got away when Baldy Krebs wounded the arresting officer. Did that by any chance happen at an *amusement* park, or was it just an ordinary public park?"

"No, an amusement park, Miss Drew."

With a growing feeling of excitement, Nancy continued, "Did either of them have any previous connection with amusement parks? I mean, for example, is that where Fingers has usually operated as a pickpocket?"

"Funny you should ask," Norris replied. "As a matter of fact, Fingers Malone was caught in that same amusement park just before he was sent to prison. You remember I told you he'd served twenty years of a twenty-five year sentence just before he broke out and became a fugitive? Well, it was really on account of that amusement park that he got sent up in the first place. I'll tell you how it happened."

Norris explained that, at the time, Fingers was being hunted for his part in a serious gangland crime, quite different from his usual specialty of picking pockets. But he had gone into hiding and could not be found.

"Then one night a prominent St. Louis businessman, a jeweler, got his pockets picked while he was at the park with his family. He was sore as the dickens and raised the roof down at headquarters. As a result, the chief of the bunco squad assigned an extra detail of detectives to patrol the park. And on the second night there, one of them spotted Fingers with his hand in a lady's purse and nabbed him right in the act!"

Detective Norris chuckled dryly over the phone and added, "Turned out Fingers had been lying low and working as a 'carny' there in the amusement park, while he waited for the heat to cool down. But he couldn't resist temptation. Those expert fingers of his turned out to be his downfall!"

After thanking both Detective Norris and Police Chief McGinnis, Nancy drove on to Joy's house in an optimistic frame of mind.

Joy herself opened the door. "I saw you coming up the drive, Nancy. I'm so glad you came!"

"I thought we might rack our brains a little more over your father's puzzle," Nancy said with a smile.

"Oh, great! I'm just in the mood!"

On entering the spacious front room, Nancy saw Joy's Aunt Selma seated in front of the television set, watching an afternoon soap opera. "Oh, good afternoon, Mrs. Yawley," she said politely.

The woman looked up and nodded coldly.

Joy took Nancy on through the house to her father's study. No sooner had she closed the door behind them than she whirled eagerly to face her visitor. "Nancy, do you think I should get in touch with that Mrs. Harrod, even though Aunt Selma forbids it?"

Nancy replied calmly, "I think you should be guided by your own conscience, Joy."

A relieved smile came over the red-haired girl's face and she clapped her hands. "Then I'm going to do it!"

She started toward the phone, only to stop short a moment before lifting the receiver. "No, on second thought, I won't do it right now. Aunt Selma might listen in on the extension—and it would be just like her to make an unpleasant fuss! I'll call later when she's out."

115

Meanwhile, Nancy had already begun drifting about the room, looking for iris clues and scrutinizing the many colorful objects with which John Trent had decorated his study.

Suddenly, Nancy snapped her fingers and exclaimed excitedly, "Joy, I think I may have found part of the answer!"

14

A Trail of Clues

"What is it, Nancy?" said Joy, flashing her an eager look. "What have you found?"

Her own eyes followed the direction of Nancy's gaze. The young detective was staring at a wall painting of a Civil War battle scene. It showed a line of blue-coated Union soldiers charging into the smoke and gunfire of a Confederate redoubt.

"Look there, Joy!" Nancy pointed at two of the figures in the painting. One, the Union color sergeant, had evidently just been hit by an enemy bullet. As he fell, a companion was snatching the flag from the dying sergeant's hand.

"Look at what?" Joy's face took on a puzzled

frown. "I mean, I see what you're pointing at—but so what?"

"That's an American flag—Old Glory."

"Oh, yes—of course! But . . . " Joy's voice trailed off uncertainly and she still looked puzzled.

The flag was rather small in the picture, and its bright stars and stripes were dimmed by the gunsmoke, so that it did not readily strike the eye at first glance. Nancy realized that she must have noticed it the first time she inspected the room, even though the impression had merely glimmered at the back of her mind and she had been unable to bring it into clear focus.

But now the flag's significance seemed obvious!

"Notice where the flagstaff is pointing." As she spoke, Nancy's finger traced an invisible line from the spearpoint at the tip of the flagstaff, across the painted canvas, and out beyond the edge of the picture frame.

The line pointed straight toward a single iris in a slender glass vase standing on a shelf close by!

"Oh!" Joy caught her breath with excitement as she realized what Nancy was getting at. "*Iris* and *Old Glory*—just like in that riddle in Daddy's letter!"

"And you did tell me, didn't you, that all the fresh irises in the house are replaced daily, by your father's standing order?"

"Yes, that's right! So this *must* be what his riddle referred to—because he knew there'd always be an iris in that vase for the flag to point at!"

Nancy nodded thoughtfully. "It certainly seems like more than a coincidence," she mused aloud, "but we still don't know what the question mark in the riddle stands for."

She was silent for several moments, then turned to her red-haired friend. "Those words— 'iris' and 'Old Glory'—what do they suggest to you, Joy? . . . Anything at all?"

Joy wrinkled her forehead and shrugged. "Not really . . . Well, wait a minute. They do remind me of something."

"Such as?" Nancy inquired keenly.

"That carousel horse I told you about. When Daddy first bought him for me as a birthday present, I named him Glory, because he was so beautiful. And sometimes, in those days, when I'd talk about him, I'd refer to him as 'Old Glory.'" Joy flashed a rueful smile. "But I guess that doesn't help much, does it?"

"Hm, you never know. You said you lent your horse to the River Heights Day-Care Center?"

"That's right. Would you like to see it?"

"Very much," declared Nancy. "Let's drive over there right now, Joy!"

"Okay, suits me."

The day-care center was located in a big, old house, not far from Riverside Park, in what had once been a neighborhood of aristocratic mansions. Two other houses in the same block were now empty, and, according to a builder's sign, were soon to be torn down to make way for an elevated parking garage, leaving the center as the only occupied site. Its grounds were overgrown with shrubbery and shaded by tall, ancient oaks and hemlocks.

Despite these rather gloomy surroundings, however, the house itself had a cheerful air and bustled with the sounds and laughter of children at play. It was staffed by volunteer members, one of whom—a Miss Blandish—greeted the two visitors cordially.

"The children are just about to have their afternoon nap," she informed Joy, "so you and Nancy will be able to look over your hobbyhorse undisturbed."

The horse stood near a big, mullioned window in what once had evidently been the mansion's game room. With its raised, prancing foreleg, arched neck, and flying mane, the carousel steed looked incredibly lifelike. Its flaring pink nostrils, fiery eyes, and glossy, dapple-gray coat all added to the vivid impression, and its feathered bridle and gilded trappings seemed to make it a truly royal charger.

"Oh, how beautiful!" Nancy murmured softly, gazing at the horse in wide-eyed admiration.

"Now you can see why I fell in love with him when I was a little girl!" said Joy, obviously pleased by her reaction. "Would you like to ride him?"

Nancy giggled. "Is anyone watching?"

"What's the diff? Go on!"

Nancy, who was wearing jeans, put one foot in a stirrup and swung herself gracefully into the saddle. As she began to post up and down on the spring-mounted hobbyhorse, the music-box mechanism in the stand tinkled out a gay, lively rendition of "Yankee Doodle."

"Oh, hey! This is great!" Nancy exclaimed.

Joy watched merrily. "Something tells me you're an expert horsewoman, Nancy!"

"I've ridden in a few shows." Chuckling, she added, "If I had a horse like Glory at home, I'd probably have no time for detecting!"

The ride and the tune ended with both girls convulsed in a fit of laughter as Nancy dismounted. Even while galloping to the music, she had been aware of some of the fine details of the horse's carving, and now that she was out of the saddle and on her feet again, she could appreciate the workmanship even more.

"You know, Joy," she mused with one finger to her lips as she gazed at the lovely steed, "Glory is not one of the original carousel horses. It's carved in a much more realistic and lifelike style."

"Well, I always knew it was more beautiful than the other horses on the merry-go-round," Joy said proudly, "but I'm not sure I ever noticed it was of different workmanship. Why? Does that have some connection with Daddy's riddle?"

"Not necessarily. But it does mean the carousel operator lied to me for some reason." Nancy explained how Leo Novak had told her the lead horse had been replaced twice: once when Joy's father bought Glory, and again when the replacement horse was damaged by a park truck.

But if Glory, too, was not one of the original carousel steeds, then the lead horse must have been replaced *three* times!

Another thought intrigued and excited Nancy. When Fingers Malone and Baldy Krebs

122

were sneakily examining the carousel horses on Monday night after the park closed, could Glory have been the one they were looking for?

Also, the burglars who broke into the Trents' house had taken nothing. Was this because the arrival of the police car had scared them off? Or could they have been looking for Joy's carousel horse, but failed to find it because it was at the day-care center?

Nancy realized that if her theorizing was right, then Glory must be valuable for some reason! . . . But *why?*

Nancy was still deep in thought as she and Joy walked away down the flagstone path leading from the old house to the street—so deeply absorbed, in fact, that she stumbled and almost fell.

"Oh, Nancy dear!" cried Joy, catching her friend by the arm. "Are you all right?"

"Yes, thanks—just stubbed my toe," Nancy said ruefully. Looking down, she saw that one of the ancient flags had tilted unevenly, so that a corner of it protruded above the ground, and this was what had caught her foot.

A startled expression came over Nancy's face as another exciting hunch flashed through her mind. "Joy, I've just thought of something!" she cried. "Let's go back to your house right away!"

As they drove through the afternoon traffic, Joy listened eagerly to Nancy's idea.

"Are you aware," the girl sleuth inquired, "that the flower called iris also has another name?"

Joy nodded. "Of course. Some people call them flags." As she uttered the last word, Joy caught on with a smile to Nancy's trend of thought. "Oh! Is that what gave you your sudden inspiration—when you stumbled back there?"

"Right! And, by the way, have you ever had algebra in school, Joy?"

"Yes, though I must admit I'm no genius at math. Why?"

"Because if you think of you father's message as a mathematical equation, it makes sense!"

Joy wrinkled her forehead. "I'm not sure I follow."

"Well, maybe I should have said it makes sense *if* you substitute the word 'flag' for the question mark—because Old Glory is also a flag," Nancy explained. "In other words, the message would then read: *Iris equals flag equals Old Glory!*"

"Of course! I get it now!" Joy exclaimed. "Oh, Nancy, how brilliant of you! So a *flag* must be the answer to Daddy's riddle!"

"Exactly! and I suspect the place to look for whatever flag he's referring to is right there in his study!"

Minutes later, the two girls were hurrying into John Trent's study. Almost at once, Nancy's attention fastened on a metal statuette. It portrayed an old-time western cavalryman of Indian-fighting days. He was mounted on horseback and carrying a banner in one hand.

The statuette, Nancy noticed, was a bronze casting. But evidently, the banner had been separately crafted. Its slender staff—which, though rigid, was not much thicker than a stout wire—passed through an opening in the rider's hand. Its lower end fitted into a socket on his saddle.

Nancy cautiously fingered the flagstaff. Despite its snug fit, she noticed that it could be jiggled slightly.

"Oh!" Joy gasped, looking on in wide-eyed suspense. "Do you think that's the flag Daddy meant?"

"We'll soon find out," Nancy prophesied. She tugged on the flagstaff, pulling it upward through the hole in the rider's hand.

As the staff came loose from its saddle socket, something else came out with it. Joy snatched the object up excitedly.

It was a tiny wad of fine tissue paper!

Both girls held their breath as Joy uncrumpled and smoothed out the tissue.

It bore a crude drawing of a horse—with a frog riding on its back!

15

The Yesterday Message

"Another riddle!" Joy exclaimed. "What on earth does it mean?"

"A frog on a horse," Nancy murmured pensively. Then she shook her head. "I'm afraid I don't know, either, Joy. But the drawing must mean *some*thing, or your father wouldn't have left it here for you to find. I'm sure we can decipher it if we put our heads together and think hard enough."

In the meantime, the statuette itself—the bronze likeness of a western cavalryman—had started a brand-new train of thought in Nancy's mind. "There's another lead on the carousel mystery that I want to check out this afternoon, Joy," she went on. "I'll let you know as soon as I have anything to report."

From the Trents' house, Nancy drove to the River Heights Public Library. There she looked up the name Walter Kruse in the catalog file. Several books were listed about the famous western artist and his work, and Nancy was able to find one of them on the shelves. It was entitled *The Art of Walter Kruse*.

She took her find to a table near the window and began leafing through its pages. As she studied the reproductions in color of Kruse's paintings and sculptures, Nancy grew more and more excited. "So my hunch was right!" she murmured under her breath. "Now I'm sure of it!"

After returning the book to its place on the shelf, Nancy went to the pay telephone in the library's front lobby and called the director of the River Heights Art Museum, who was an old friend. They spoke for several minutes. Then she hung up and called reporter Rick Jason at the *News*.

"Hi, Nancy!" he said. "How are you coming on the carousel mystery?"

"I think I'm getting close to a solution, but I'll need your help. Would you do me a favor?"

"Just name it!"

Nancy told him about Joy Trent's carousel horse at the day-care center and asked if he could arrange to have a picture story about it appear in the evening paper. "I know it's late to be asking," she added apologetically, "but this is really important. It may pay off in quite a news scoop if I do succeed in solving the mystery."

"Okay. We're almost ready to go to press, so we may have to remake a couple of pages to fit it in, but that's no great problem. I'll talk to the editor and get a photographer on the job pronto."

"Another thing," Nancy went on hastily. "Could your editor possibly use his influence with the television news people to get a similar story broadcast on tonight's news? You know—about how a horse from the haunted carousel has turned up at the local day-care center?"

"One can but try," Rick Jason replied. "If I pass the word that it may help Nancy Drew solve the carousel mystery, I think they'll probably go along. But remember—I get the scoop."

The teenage sleuth chuckled. "That's a promise. And thanks a million for your help!"

Hanging up, Nancy hurried out of the library to her car and headed for Bess Marvin's house. Bess told her that Ned Nickerson had been trying to reach her.

"Okay, thanks, Bess—I'll call him," Nancy responded. "But first, how would you like to help me out on a little detective work at the park?"

Bess's blue eyes lit up with suppressed excitement. "Need you ask? . . . I mean—well, providing it's not too dangerous."

Nancy dimpled. "Don't worry—no more crook chases. At least, not if I can help it!"

She explained hastily what she had in mind. Then she called Ned and arranged to meet him at Riverside Park. Moments later, the two girls were whizzing there in Nancy's trim, blue sports car.

On arriving, Nancy stayed behind in the car, according to their prearranged plan, while Bess made her way on foot to the carousel. There she stopped and began watching the merry-go-round revolve gaily with its riders, as if she were waiting for someone. Every few minutes she would walk about restlessly and take up a new position, just to make sure the operator noticed her.

Leo Novak had seen Bess Marvin before, and soon recognized her as Nancy Drew's chum. "Waiting for your friend?" he asked presently.

"Yes—for Nancy Drew." Bess pretended to be in a chatty mood and began boasting about Nancy's many successes as a sleuth. "Incidentally, I guess you won't have to worry anymore about your carousel being haunted!"

"Oh no?" Novak tilted an eyebrow. "How come?"

"Well, this is off the record, you understand, but Nancy told me she found a hobbyhorse at the River Heights Day-Care Center, which originally came off your *Wonderland Gallop*."

"Is that so? One of Mr. Ogden's old carousel horses, huh?" Novak's expression took on a shrewd frown as he added, "What's that got to do with the haunting, though?"

Bess shrugged her plump shoulders. "Search me, but that's what Nancy told me. I believe she thinks that whoever was playing such a prank on you was really searching for that horse—and now that it's turned up, the prank won't be necessary anymore. If there's no more haunting, she says, that will prove her theory's correct."

"Hmph." Novak grunted in a way that sounded as if he was not convinced. "Sounds pretty far out to me."

Several minutes later, Nancy came walking toward the merry-go-round to join Bess. On seeing Nancy, the carousel operator said, "Your girlfriend's been telling me you've figured out why my carousel plays at night."

Nancy smiled politely. "Well, let's say I have a theory about it."

"She also claims there won't be any more of this spooky business."

"Only if my theory's right."

Leo Novak continued to ply Nancy with questions, obviously fishing for information, but she fended them off with a few teasing remarks. Then Nancy turned to her chum. "Come on, Bess—it's past five. We'd better be getting back to the car."

As the two girls walked off, Novak stared after them with an irritated look of frustration.

Ned Nickerson was waiting beside Nancy's blue sports car when she and Bess reached the parking lot. "Still hard at work on the mystery trail?"

Nancy grinned back at her boyfriend. "Just testing a theory, you might say. Care to come on an errand with me?"

"Sure. Whereabouts?"

"The Regent Hotel. But I promised Bess I'd drive her home first."

Ned followed the girls in his own car. Then, after going to her own house and parking in the driveway, Nancy slid in beside him. On their way to the hotel, she related the strange way in which the mystery woman, Mrs. Rose Harrod, had sent an iris to Joy Trent.

"I want to let her know that Joy Trent intends to get in touch with her," Nancy ended.

The Regent Hotel, though rather small and old-fashioned in its decor, was one of the most exclusive hotels in River Heights. Nancy first tried to call Mrs. Harrod's room on one of the house phones in the lobby. But no one answered, so she sought help from the desk clerk.

"Would you happen to know, by any chance, where Mrs. Harrod has gone, or how soon she'll be back?"

"I couldn't say, miss. But let me check her room slot." The clerk turned to the honeycomb of numbered cubbyholes behind the marble-topped counter. "Well, her room key's here, so she's evidently out somewhere. Let's see what this note says."

He glanced at the slip of paper that he pulled out of the 922 cubbyhole. "Hm, that's odd," he murmured and handed it to Nancy.

The paper was the kind of form slip on which clerks jotted down messages to or from the hotel guests. It said:

TIME. *5:45 P.M.*
MESSAGE. *If Nancy Drew or Joy Trent phones or comes to hotel, please tell them I had to go out to airport but will be back shortly.*

Mrs. Harrod

Nancy looked up and saw the puzzled expression on the desk clerk's face. "Is something wrong?"

"I'm not sure. . . ." He scratched his head uncertainly and turned to glance up at the wall clock overhead. "It's now going on six, and I've been on duty for the past few hours—but I know *I* didn't write that message. So it must have been left in the slot yesterday."

Nancy caught her breath anxiously. "Then you—you mean Mrs. Harrod's been *missing for the past twenty-four hours?!*"

16

Kidnap Car

"Well, I don't know if 'missing' is the right word," the clerk replied cautiously, "but it does seem as though she hasn't returned to the hotel."

Seeing Nancy's dismayed look, he went on, "Tell you what, the relief clerk—the one who must have taken down that message—will be coming on duty shortly. He can tell you more about it than I can." The desk clerk smiled reassuringly.

"Yes, of course. I'll wait for him," Nancy said, realizing nothing could be done until then. She went and sat next to Ned on a sofa amid the lobby's potted palms and tried to curb her impatience. Finally, after ten long minutes, a

135

dark-haired young man walked behind the counter, buttoning his uniform jacket.

As Nancy rose and walked to the desk, she kept her fingers crossed. It turned out that she was in luck. The young man had a good memory.

"Sure, I remember writing down that message," he recalled. "Mrs. Harrod dictated it to me. Some man had called her just a couple of minutes before."

"Did the caller leave his name?" Nancy inquired.

"No, but he had rung her room and gotten no answer, so his call was switched here to the desk. It was about that girl whose name is on the message—Joy Trent." The clerk pointed to the slip of paper on the marble counter.

"Do you mind telling me what the caller wanted?"

"No, he said that if Mrs. Harrod wanted some information about this Joy Trent, she should meet him at the airport coffee shop—that he'd wait for her there exactly one hour. And she should look for a man with a mustache and a cane."

The desk clerk went on to relate that just as he had hung up from taking this call, Mrs. Harrod herself had come walking into the lobby. "I told her what the man had said, and it seemed to make her very happy. That's when she dictated this message to me—and I stuck it in her room slot as a reminder. Then she turned right around and left the hotel again. Since her room key's still here, I guess she never came back."

"Thanks ever so much for your help." Nancy smiled at the desk clerk, trying not to show her worry. Then she went back to the sofa to tell Ned what she had learned.

"We'd better get out to the airport!" said Ned. Nancy nodded, and they hurried outside to his car.

The airport was not far from River Heights, but in the rush-hour traffic the going seemed agonizingly slow. After Ned had parked his car in the airport lot, the two young people quickly made their way to the coffee shop inside the air terminal.

There was a serving counter and small tables grouped around the shop's glass window-walls. Aside from a middle-aged woman nibbling a sandwich at one of the tables, the place was empty.

As Nancy and Ned hesitated uncertainly, a smiling, kindly-looking woman in a waitress uniform emerged from the kitchen. She was

137

carrying some boxes which she put under the counter.

"Can I help you people?"

In response, Nancy described Rose Harrod and the time when she had presumably come to the coffee shop yesterday.

The waitress nodded promptly with a look of interest. "Yes, I remember her. It was almost as quiet as today. She came in and looked around and went right to that table over there." The waitress pointed. "Some guy was sitting there— must've been waiting for her, I guess. Anyhow, he ordered fresh coffee for himself and a cup for her, and they began talking."

"This man she met," Nancy interrupted, "can you describe him?"

"Yeah, he was kind of a skinny old guy . . . had a mustache and glasses and a hook nose . . . oh, and I remember he had a cane."

"Please go on."

"Well, next time I looked over that way, the lady had her elbows on the table, and she was holding her head in her hands. She looked real sick."

Nancy exchanged a startled glance with Ned, who asked the waitress, "Sick enough to need medical attention?"

"She sure looked that way to me. The old guy threw some bills on the table, and they left. She was so wobbly he had to help her walk."

"Did anyone send for an ambulance?" Nancy inquired.

"No, I could see right out through the glass. A big, fat guy with long, blond hair and a beard came up and offered to help. He was holding the lady on one side. I ran out to give the old man his change and ask if I could call a doctor."

"What did he say?"

"He said he was a doctor himself, and he'd take her out for some fresh air." The waitress shrugged. "So they walked out of the building, and that's the last I saw of them. How come you're looking for her, dear? Was the lady a relative of yours?"

"No, just a—a friend. But she never returned to her hotel, so it's quite worrisome."

The waitress clucked sympathetically. Nancy thanked her for the information and went back out to the parking lot with Ned.

"I hate to say this, Nancy, but it sounds like Mrs. Harrod was drugged," Ned commented.

"That's just what I'm afraid of. That man she met could easily have slipped something into her coffee." Nancy shaded her eyes as she gazed at the row of parked cars. "Ned, Rose

Harrod's car was a silver two-door sedan—I don't know what make, but I'm sure I'll recognize it. Let's see if it's still in the lot."

After several minutes of searching, Nancy sighed. "Wow, I never realized it before, but silver has got to to be the most popular car color!"

"Let's talk to the parking lot attendant," Ned suggested.

"Yes, maybe he'll remember," Nancy said. "Let's just hope he was on duty this time yesterday."

The attendant was reading a newspaper in his booth. He was a chubby man about fifty years old, and was a retired policeman. When Nancy asked him about Mrs. Harrod, he immediately recalled seeing the two men bring her into the lot from the air terminal the day before.

"Reason I remember is, she drove in here in a nice-looking silver car, and then ten or fifteen minutes later she comes back out, with two guys having to hold her up on her feet. And then she leaves in their car, instead of her own. 'Course I could see she'd been taken ill, but even so it seemed kinda odd."

"Did you talk to them at all?"

"Well, when they drove up to pay me, I asked her if everything was okay—at least I tried to—I mean about leaving her car here and all. She was too sick and woozy to give me a straight answer, but the old guy with glasses and a mustache said he was a doctor and he was taking her to the hospital."

Nancy said, "Do you remember what kind of a car he was driving?"

"Yeah, a beat-up old black station wagon. That seemed funny too, 'cause I figured a doctor would be driving a better car than that. So I even wrote down the license number—just in case. I got it right here."

"Good for you!" Nancy jotted down the information which the parking lot attendant supplied, then thanked him and hurried to the nearest public telephone with Ned.

Nancy called Police Chief McGinnis and gave him the description and license number of the station wagon. She asked if he could trace its registration and have all police cars keep a lookout for it.

"Will do, Nancy. I'll call as soon as I have anything," Chief McGinnis promised.

After hanging up, Nancy said, "Would you like to come to dinner with me, Ned? There's nothing more we can do for the time being, and I'm sure you must be as hungry as I am."

"Sounds good to me!" Ned replied with a

grin. Soon they were on their way to the Drews' house.

Hannah Gruen was just about to serve dinner. The motherly housekeeper set another place for Ned, and the two young people joined her and Mr. Drew at the table.

Nancy had just finished her shrimp cocktail when the telephone rang. She immediately jumped up, saying, "That may be for me—I'll get it."

"Nancy?" said the caller's voice when she picked up. "Chief McGinnis here. Sorry if this is your dinner hour, but I thought you'd want to know immediately. That station wagon was reported stolen yesterday. It was found abandoned, early this morning, out near Fishwick. Hope this helps you."

"Oh, it does, Chief. Thanks for letting me know so promptly."

Hanging up, Nancy returned quickly to the dining room. "Ned, they found the station wagon out near Fishwick this morning. I'm going out there now. Want to come?"

"Sure thing. Please excuse me, Mrs. Gruen—Mr. Drew." He rose from the table.

Nancy hastily apologized for interrupting the meal. "Dad, Hannah—I'll explain it all when we get back. It's really urgent—I'm sorry.

Please go on with your dinner. We'll get something later on, while we're out."

Nancy kissed her father, gave Hannah a hug, and whirled out of the room, followed by Ned.

It was not yet 8:00 P.M. and still light out. Fortunately traffic was sparse, and Nancy drove as fast as the speed limit allowed down to the River Road, then out along the two-lane country road that led to Fishwick.

"I feel I just can't get there fast enough, Ned," Nancy murmured anxiously. "What do you think happened to her?"

"I don't know. Maybe we should have checked the hospitals first."

"You're right. If this turns out to be a fruitless trip, that's the next thing we'll do."

Fishwick was a seedy beach community strung out along the riverbank. It centered on a café, a gas station and general store, and a boating pier. A row of run-down-looking cottages completed the picture.

After slowing to look around, Nancy pulled into the gas station. A leathery-faced man got up off his tilted-back chair. "What'll it be—gas or bait?"

"Neither." Nancy smiled at him. "You look like a very observant man."

The man responded with a pleased grin and

shrewd wink. "Ain't much goes on around here gets by me. Why? You lookin' for someone?"

"Yes, a sick woman. Two men brought her out here late yesterday in an old, black station wagon. Did you happen to notice them?"

"Yep—that's the place." He pointed to a cottage half hidden among some trees.

"Do you know who lives there?"

"Shucks, can't keep track. These places are rented by the day or week."

Nancy thanked him and drove on with Ned to the cottage. When they knocked, no one answered. But suddenly, a faint moan reached their ears.

"Ned, did you hear that?!" Nancy exclaimed.

"You bet I did!" Her friend put his husky shoulder to the door and pushed hard.

The cheap lock soon gave way, and the door flew open. Nancy gasped at the sight that met their eyes.

On a bare cot lay Rose Harrod, tied and gagged!

17

Double Stakeout

Nancy rushed to undo the woman's gag. "Mrs. Harrod!" she exclaimed. "Are you all right?"

The woman's eyes flickered open, but they scarcely seemed to focus, and the only audible response was a few faint, mumbled words. "I . . . I d-don't know . . . Wh-where am I?"

Before Nancy could reply, Rose Harrod's eyes rolled upward and her lids drooped shut again. She was obviously dazed and disoriented.

"She must still be under the effects of that drug the fellow gave her!" Ned declared grimly.

But Nancy shook her head. "I doubt if whatever he slipped in her coffee would keep her under this long. More likely they sedated her again after they brought her here to the cottage."

The cottage, though barely furnished, at least had electricity and running water. Ned switched on the overhead light, since dusk was gathering fast outside, and untied the ropes binding Mrs. Harrod. Meanwhile, Nancy wrung out her handkerchief in cold water.

Together, they raised Rose Harrod to a sitting position and managed to revive her. But she was able to stammer out only a few confused words about the kidnapping before slumping unconscious again.

"We'd better get her to a doctor right away," Ned decided.

"Yes, the sooner the better," Nancy agreed. "I'll help you carry her out to the car."

"No problem. I can carry her."

Ned, a well-muscled six-footer, easily gathered the woman up in his arms, and minutes later they were speeding back to town.

After they had delivered Mrs. Harrod to the emergency room of the River Heights Hospital, Nancy called police headquarters to report what had happened. By the time she hung up, the intern on duty had finished examining the patient.

"She's been drugged, all right," he told Nancy and Ned, "but I don't think there'll be any permanent ill effects. In any case, I want to keep her here under observation, at least overnight."

The two young people went to a nearby restaurant to settle down at last to their delayed dinner. But both were still too keyed up over the events of the evening to eat much. Moreover, Nancy was already laying plans for her night's detective work.

"Will you help me, Ned?" she asked. When he eagerly agreed, Nancy explained what she had in mind. Then she made several calls from a pay telephone in the rest room. She succeeded in contacting reporter Rick Jason; George's friend Neil Sawyer, the electrical engineering student; and the park policeman, Officer Doyle, who by now had gone off duty. All three promised to meet her shortly before 11:00 P.M. at the same wooded stakeout spot where she and Ned had kept watch on the carousel on Monday night.

It was long past nine-thirty when Nancy and Ned finally left the restaurant. They drove first to police headquarters, where Nancy borrowed a pair of police walkie-talkie radios. Then they drove on to the Trents' house. Nancy had already called Joy from the restaurant and learned that she had a key to the day-care center, since Joy did volunteer work there in addition to lending her carousel horse for the children's enjoyment.

Ned waited in the car while Nancy went up to ring the bell. Joy herself answered the door and handed Nancy the key.

"Something tells me you have an exciting evening ahead," she said enviously.

The young sleuth chuckled and held up crossed fingers. "I just hope it doesn't get too exciting for my health!"

After leaving Joy's house, Nancy and Ned headed for the day-care center. They parked well out of sight of their destination and walked the rest of the way.

At this late hour, the whole surrounding neighborhood lay dark and silent. The only sounds were an occasional faint echo of traffic from Riverside Avenue, which bordered the park, several blocks away. Nancy and Ned found a shadowy spot among the tall pines and hemlocks and bushes from which they could keep watch unseen on the big, old house.

During dinner, they had found time to glance at the photo story on the center's carousel horse which had appeared in the evening paper.

"You think that'll be enough to attract the same burglars who broke into Joy Trent's house?" Ned inquired softly.

"That or the television news bit, I hope," Nancy replied, "assuming my hunch is right, of course."

As the hands of her wristwatch crept around toward eleven o'clock, Nancy finally left Ned to keep watch alone while she went to check with her three cohorts outside the amusement park.

Rick Jason, Neil Sawyer, and Officer Doyle were all waiting at the agreed-upon spot just outside the park's pipe-and-chain barrier as Nancy came walking along the dark footpath to join them.

Rick Jason was in high spirits at the prospect of a possible news scoop. "So this is how the famous girl detective gets her man, eh?" he bantered.

Nancy's blue eyes twinkled in the moonlight. "That remains to be seen."

Minutes later, the midway lights were turned off, and the amusement park area gradually settled down to stillness and darkness. At last, Neil Sawyer legged over the pipe-chain barrier and made his way cautiously toward the carousel.

When he returned, he was grinning broadly.

"Did my ploy work?" Nancy inquired.

"You bet! There's a radio-relay switch attached to the control box, just like I described to you!" he reported with a triumphant look.

"Marvelous!" Nancy grinned back. "George certainly recommended the right technical expert!"

After a hasty final discussion with Neil, Rick, and Officer Doyle, Nancy left the park and returned to Ned at their spy post outside the day-care center.

"Any developments, Ned?"

"Nothing so far. I just wish we'd brought something comfortable to sit on!"

Nancy giggled softly. "Never mind, at least there's enough grass and undergrowth to keep the pine needles from pricking us!"

She leaned against her friend's shoulder, and Ned slipped his arm around her waist. Twenty minutes went by pleasantly as they chatted under their breath and enjoyed each other's company.

Suddenly there was a crackle of radio static, and Officer Doyle's voice came over Nancy's walkie-talkie: *The trap has been sprung!*

18

Circling Shadows

So her plan had succeeded! Nancy smiled triumphantly at a grinning Ned.

"Nice going, beautiful!" he commented.

Patting his arm, Nancy murmured, "I'll be back as soon as I can. Take care!"

With that, she hurried off to her car and drove the few blocks to the amusement park, which was now partially lit up. Grouped around the carousel were Officer Doyle, Rick Jason, Neil Sawyer, and a nervous-looking Leo Novak.

"Smart girl, Nancy!" Rick Jason greeted her with a grin. "Everything happened just as you predicted. The carousel suddenly started playing. That woke up the people in the trailers, and the lights came on."

"Then Mr. Novak came running up to the carousel," Officer Doyle chimed in. "It stopped playing when he was halfway to it, but he checked over the machinery."

The teenage sleuth turned to Leo Novak and asked, "What did you find?"

"Nothing, absolutely nothing!" the carousel owner blurted emphatically. He plowed his fingers through his dark hair with a bewildered expression on his face. "I have no idea what's causing all this funny business. And I don't see any sign that the operating machinery's been tampered with."

Nancy, Rick, and Officer Doyle glanced at one another. Meanwhile, Neil Sawyer quietly went over and slipped his hand under the operator's control box.

"Mr. Novak's right," he reported a moment later. "There are no gimmicks on the controls now."

In this way, he let the others know that someone had removed the radio relay he had discovered earlier that evening.

Nancy nodded and flashed a barely perceptible eye signal to Officer Doyle. The policeman immediately turned to Leo Novak.

"I wonder if you'd be good enough to empty out your pockets, sir."

"What?!" Leo Novak stared indignantly.

"It's up to you, Mr. Novak. Empty your pockets now voluntarily, or I intend to arrest you for disturbing the peace."

"Disturbing the peace?!" The owner's face was rapidly taking on a deep crimson flush.

"That's right," Officer Doyle explained calmly, "by running your carousel after hours. That'll mean a trip to the station house and everything else that goes with being arrested."

"Now wait a minute . . . !" Leo Novak began angrily. But after one look at the faces of the surrounding witnesses, he dropped his bluff and sullenly emptied his pockets.

Among the sparse contents which he dumped into Officer Doyle's waiting hands was a little metal and plastic device with a short length of wire and a spring clip attached to each end.

"There's the radio relay," said Neil Sawyer.

Next, something that looked like a small hand-held walkie-talkie with a disappearing antenna emerged from the owner's pocket.

"And there's the signal transmitter," Neil added.

Novak's face was livid with fury, but he knew he was trapped.

Nancy turned to Rick Jason. "Well, have I solved the mystery of the haunted carousel or not?"

153

Before the reporter could do more than nod, the borrowed walkie-talkie attached to Officer Doyle's belt suddenly came to life. Ned's voice, low but quivering with suppressed excitement, crackled from the speaker:

"Nancy, come back here fast . . . and try to avoid being seen!"

Leaving the policeman to deal with Leo Novak, Nancy, with a hasty wave of her hand, turned and ran back to her car in the parking lot.

In a few moments, she was driving through the dark, sleeping streets toward the day-care center. Again parking a block or so away, she slipped out of the car and walked swiftly to Ned's hiding place among the trees and shrubbery.

As she joined him, he whispered, "I saw a car drive slowly around the block three times. Then it stopped around the corner out of sight."

"Did anyone get out?" Nancy inquired softly.

"Yes, I heard a car door open and shut. And I think someone's trying to get in the house right now, by the back way!"

As the young people strained their eyes to pierce the midnight gloom, a flickering light suddenly appeared, first in one window, then another. Someone was moving through the big, old house!

"What now?" Ned said tensely. "Want me to

go in there after them?"

"We'll both go—but not yet. First we'd better make sure they didn't post a lookout."

Slipping through the trees as silently as shadows, the pair circled the grounds of the day-care center and made their way cautiously toward the marauders' car. It was empty.

Nancy drew a sigh of relief. "Okay, no lookout! Now to see what they're up to inside."

"Wait a minute!" Ned seized her arm. "Let me go in there alone. You wait out here!"

Nancy pressed her lips to his cheek. "Don't be silly—we'll be safer if we stay together!"

Before Ned could object any further, Nancy darted back toward the house. Her friend followed hastily. Hand in hand, they tiptoed up the broad front porch steps.

Nancy reached in her pocket and took out the key Joy Trent had given her. She inserted it in the lock, turned it, and cautiously pushed open the big front door. It swung inward with faintly creaking hinges. Inside, all was dark.

Nancy and Ned held their breath for a moment to make sure no one had heard the creaks. Then they slipped into the house and inched the door shut behind them.

Having visited the day-care center many hours earlier, Nancy fortunately was able to lead the way. Groping for obstacles in the darkness, they crossed a tiled vestibule, then went down a central hall and veered off through two carpeted rooms toward what was now the nursery playroom.

Here, they paused and, with bated breath, maneuvered themselves into suitable positions from which to peek into the lighted playroom.

Two men were standing near Joy's carousel horse. One was a thin, scar-faced elderly fellow in a dark business suit with glasses, mustache, and a large hooked nose. The other, who looked like an overage hippie, was big and fat with long, blond hair and a beard.

They appeared to be tampering with the saddle pad of the wooden horse, trying to pry it up—first on one side, then on the other—but without success.

"You sure you got the instructions right?" the bigger man growled at his partner. "Read the letter again!"

The elderly scar-faced man took a folded paper from his pocket and started to read it aloud in a low, muttering voice. Nancy, much to her vexation, was unable to catch most of the words.

Meanwhile, Ned was leaning on the back of a chair, while he craned to peer around the edge

156

of the archway into the playroom. Suddenly, he felt his fingers slipping.

He struggled desperately to keep his grip and his balance, but it was no use. A moment later, the chair slipped out from under him, and Ned went crashing to the floor!

With a snarl and an oath, the two intruders realized they were being spied on. They rushed at Ned and Nancy!

The elderly mustached man grabbed Nancy by the shoulder. He pushed her back against the wall, pinning her tightly.

Before Ned could scramble to his feet to help her, the burly hippie booted him down again with a hard, vicious kick!

19

A Precious Parcel

Ned grabbed the crook's foot to keep from
being kicked again. He tried to twist his ankle
and topple him at the same time. The crook
started to fall, but managed to clutch on to the
chair Ned had overturned. He swung it side-
ways with both hands, grazing Ned's shoulder
and arm. Out of the corner of her eye, Nancy
saw her boyfriend wince with pain and let go
his grip on his enemy's foot.

At the same time, Nancy saw the distraction
in her captor's eye. His grip loosened, and she
shoved him backwards. She bolted forward,
snatching up one of the small, child-sized
chairs in the playroom and began to swing it at
her mustached assailant.

With an angry oath, he backed away. Although Nancy kept him at bay, she soon found she was being expertly maneuvered into a corner.

She caught a fleeting glimpse of Ned. By now, he had regained his feet and was fighting back gamely against his burly foe. But he was using only one arm and, with a sinking heart, Nancy realized it was only a matter of time before they might both find themselves at the mercy of their ruthless attackers.

Suddenly, a third man rushed into the room. At first, Nancy took it for granted that he must be an ally or partner of the other two crooks. Her hasty glance in the dim light registered only the fact that he was stocky and gray-haired and wore a clay-colored safari jacket. She tried not to panic at the thought that, with this additional help for their enemies, she and Ned would now probably be overpowered in short order.

Instead, to Nancy's astonishment, the newcomer grabbed one arm of her assailant and twisted it behind his back. As he bent forward, trying to wrench himself away, Nancy knocked him to the floor with a blow of the chair which she had been using as a shield. The crook groaned and went limp, too stunned to resist further.

Without a word, Nancy and her rescuer

turned to help Ned. His attacker grunted and gulped as the gray-haired man grabbed him around the neck. Ned seized his chance to plant his fist in the big crook's stomach. Then, as the fellow crumpled, Ned laid him a hard punch on his jaw!

With a cry of relief, Nancy hugged her friend. "Oh, Ned . . . thank goodness!" was all she could say for a moment.

"Are you all right?" he asked anxiously.

Nancy smiled up at him. "I will be . . . when I catch my breath!"

Nancy had already deduced the identities of their two attackers, partly from their voices. Their present appearances confirmed her guess. The burly hippie had lost his blond wig, and his fake beard was hanging loose. Nancy easily recognized him as Baldy Krebs. As a result of the frantic struggle, his companion's mustache and putty nose were both crooked, and the reddish fake scar had partly rubbed off his cheek when he fell to the floor.

No wonder Bess didn't recognize him as Fingers Malone after I chased him in the park that day, thought Nancy. He probably put on his disguise before he came out of the Haunted House!

Meanwhile, Ned was shaking hands with the gray-haired man in the safari jacket. Nancy, too, started to thank him—then broke off with a gasp as she got her first good look at their rescuer.

"Why, Mr. Franz, what are you doing here?" she blurted out as she recognized the retired businessman and amusement-park buff.

"Luckily, you left your key in the door just now," Franz chuckled. Turning serious, he added, "I must apologize for deceiving you, Miss Drew. Actually, I'm an insurance investigator, and I've been trailing these crooks ever since Fingers Malone broke out of prison."

"An insurance company after a crook for a prison break?" Ned looked puzzled. "I don't get it."

"It wasn't the prison break that brought him here," Nancy deduced. "I'll bet you're looking for something Fingers stole twenty years ago—right, Mr, Franz?"

It was the insurance investigator's turn to look startled. "Absolutely right, Miss Drew. But how did you know?"

"Because I learned his background from a St. Louis police detective, who's also in town looking for him."

Arno Franz explained that he had seen and heard the news stories about the carousel horse at the day-care center and, like Nancy, had suspected this might prove an irresistible bait to the criminal he was after. Accordingly, he had come to the day-care center late at night, arriving just before Nancy and Ned entered the big, old house.

Franz eyed the wooden steed in perplexity. "You know, I have a strong hunch that what I'm looking for may be hidden inside this thing," he mused aloud. "But don't ask me exactly how or where!"

Nancy smiled mysteriously. "I'll try to answer that question tomorrow, when everyone can be here," she said, "especially Joy Trent, who owns this carousel horse. In the meantime, I think we'd better let Police Chief McGinnis and Detective Norris know about these two. I'll go and phone them from the office in the next room."

A police cruiser soon arrived outside the house, and the two crooks were whisked off in handcuffs. Nancy was praised and congratulated for the clever way in which she had brought the manhunt to a successful conclusion. But the complete solution of the case still remained unknown.

When Nancy walked into the playroom at the day-care center at eleven o'clock the following morning, accompanied by Bess and George, she found an expectant group of people seated and eagerly awaiting her revelations. Among them were Arno Franz, Police Chief McGinnis, reporter Rick Jason, Detective Norris, a smiling Joy Trent, and her haughty Aunt Selma.

Bess and George found chairs next to Ned, who had arrived a few minutes earlier in his own car. "I'm dying of curiosity, Nancy!" Bess whispered to her friend. "Hurry up and start explaining!"

Nancy smiled and cleared her throat. "We've had a number of mysterious happenings in River Heights recently, but one way or another they all have to do with this carousel horse of Joy's—which, incidentally, happens to be extremely valuable."

Joy Trent shot a quizzical glance at the young detective. "Glory certainly means a lot to me, Nancy," she said, "but you mean he's valuable for some other reason, too?"

"Very much so. He was carved by a famous western artist named Walter Kruse, and the director of the River Heights Art Museum estimates your horse may be worth a great deal—thousands of dollars, in fact!"

Joy's eyes widened, and the audience gasped at Nancy's announcement. The teenage detective explained that horses had been one of Kruse's favorite subjects, as both a painter and a sculptor, and that she had easily identified his style after consulting the library book that contained pictures of his work.

"When Kruse carved this horse," Nancy went on, "he was an unknown artist. At the time, he was working as a carny roustabout at the same amusement park in St. Louis where the *Wonderland Gallop* was located. The lead horse on the carousel was damaged by a truck. So as a favor to his girlfriend's father, who then owned the merry-go-round, Walter Kruse carved a replacement horse."

"No wonder it's so beautiful!" Bess murmured.

Nancy related that Leo Novak was only an employee of the owner, Mr. Ogden, when the horse was carved. Later, Ogden moved the carousel to River Heights, but after several years he took it back to the same amusement park in St. Louis. On Ogden's death, Novak took over the *Wonderland Gallop*.

"Then last winter," Nancy went on, "Novak read a newspaper story about the late artist, Walter Kruse, and how his work was now bringing record prices in New York art galleries. He suddenly realized that this was the same Walter Kruse who had carved the replacement horse for the carousel which Ogden had sold to Joy's father—and if he could get it back, it might be worth a small fortune."

Unfortunately for Novak, however, he had been unable to recall the name of the little girl or her father. So he devised a clever plan and moved the carousel back to River Heights.

"By playing the carousel spookily at night," said Nancy, "Novak gained a lot of free publicity for the *Wonderland Gallop*—which, of course, also helped to make it a popular attraction at the amusement park. But his real purpose was to make sure Joy heard that the carousel had returned to River Heights. He was hoping that the news might draw her out to the park for a nostalgic visit. If so, he was sure he would recognize her by her flaming red hair and different-colored eyes—especially since he still had the photograph of her as a little girl that Mr. Trent had presented to Ogden at the time. It's still stuck up on the wall of the trailer that Novak took over when he bought the carousel."

Fingers Malone and Baldy Krebs, however, had spoiled Novak's plan. They, too, were after the horse which Kruse had carved—for a different reason. They were the two dark figures seen by Ned and Nancy the night they kept watch in the park. After failing to find what they were looking for that night, they realized that a new lead horse had been mounted on the merry-go-round. So they came to Leo's trailer later on that same night, and scared the truth out of him. He knew the two wanted criminals were highly dangerous, so he told them the whole story of how the horse had been bought by Joy's father.

But next day, Nancy went on, when they saw Detective Norris from St. Louis hunting them at the park, they jumped to the conclusion that Leo Novak had betrayed them to the police. So they beat him up as a warning and gave him a black eye. When Joy came to the park, they trailed her home and returned that night to break into the Trent house, but failed to find the horse. Novak, guessing what they would do, had vengefully tipped off the police, but Fingers and Baldy managed to escape capture.

"If you'll excuse me for interrupting, Nancy," Rick Jason cut in, "you still haven't told us why those two crooks—Fingers Malone and Baldy Krebs—were after Joy's horse."

Nancy smiled. "I was just coming to that. The reason goes back twenty years to a time when Fingers was first being hunted by the law. He was hiding out in that same St. Louis amusement park where the *Wonderland Gallop* was situated—working as a carny—but he couldn't resist picking pockets. He even persuaded one of the young park employees to help him on occasion. Detective Norris says he was arrested the other day."

The St. Louis officer nodded, then told the

history of Fingers Malone, beginning with a prominent local jeweler who had been robbed at the park. The loot was a small parcel of diamonds which he had just received from New York that afternoon. Fingers Malone was nabbed soon afterward, but the diamonds were never recovered.

"In fact," said Nancy, "the insurance company that Mr. Arno Franz works for has been trying to trace those diamonds ever since."

"Do you know what happened to them?" Rick Jason inquired keenly.

Nancy smiled and nodded. "I think so. Fingers knew he might soon be arrested, so he entrusted the diamonds to his friend, Walt Kruse."

"You mean a famous artist helped this pickpocket hide his loot?"

"Remember, Kruse wasn't a famous artist yet at that time," Nancy pointed out. "As a matter of fact, he was quite a rough-and-ready, happy-go-lucky type—an ex-cowboy and cattle rustler, who didn't give a hoot for the law. Mind you, I'm not saying he knew the parcel Fingers gave him contained stolen goods. He simply didn't ask any questions and agreed to keep the jewels."

Soon afterward, Nancy continued, an art dealer saw some of Kruse's work and invited him to come to New York and pursue his career.

As an impish joke, Kruse decided to hide the diamonds inside the carousel horse, which he had just about finished carving for his girl-friend's father. By then, Fingers had been arrested and placed on trial. Kruse, however, managed to get word to him through a confidential letter smuggled to him in the courtroom by a friend.

"As a result," Nancy concluded, "Fingers went looking for the loot when he broke out of prison twenty years later."

"And I've been trailing him ever since," said Arno Franz. "But if Fingers received Kruse's letter, why couldn't he and Baldy find the diamonds in the horse last night?"

"Because," Nancy replied with a twinkling glance at Joy, "they didn't know that John Trent had already found the diamonds when he re-mounted the horse on a stand of his own design!"

"*What?!*" Joy looked astounded. "But, Nancy, Daddy never said a word to me about finding any such thing!"

"No, I think he kept them as a surprise for you, Joy—along with another surprise."

20

Picture Story

"*Another* surprise?" Joy gave Nancy a bewildered stare and giggled nervously. "I'd say there've been enough surprises already to . . . oh, wait!" she broke off eagerly. "Does this one have something to do with that drawing we found tucked in the statuette in Daddy's study?"

"Good guess, Joy. Do you have it with you?"

"Oh yes, of course!" With trembling fingers, Joy fished the crumpled piece of tissue paper out of her bag and handed it to the teenage sleuth.

Nancy showed the drawing to her audience, all of whom were watching and listening with intense fascination as she unraveled the tangled mystery. "As you see, it's a drawing of a frog on a horse. For a long time, I couldn't imagine what it might mean . . . until I suddenly realized that there *is* a frog on every horse—in fact *four* of them!"

"Four frogs on every horse?" Police Chief McGinnis scratched his balding head. "You'll have to explain that to the rest of us who aren't expert riders like you, Nancy."

Nancy grinned back and explained. "The tough, spongy part in the center of a horse's foot, I mean the part enclosed by the hard hoof, is called the 'frog.'"

Nancy gestured toward the carousel horse. "Since Glory is a lead horse rather than a jumper, he has three feet on the ground and only one upraised. So I'm sure that Mr. Trent's sketch of a frog on a horse was intended to draw Joy's attention to this one particular foot."

Nancy's brow puckered slightly. "In Glory's case, of course, his whole foot and leg are made of wood, so . . . No, wait a minute!" An excited look came over Nancy's face as she pressed hard on the bottom of the horse's upraised hoof. "The frog on this foot is *not* wood—it feels more like hard rubber!"

She broke off long enough to get a nail file from her shoulder bag, then returned to her examination of Glory's foot. The glossy paint made it appear that the horseshoe, hoof, and frog were all made of wood. But when Nancy ran the point of her nail file around the inside curve of the horseshoe and then began to gouge and pry as deeply as she could, it gradually became apparent that the frog had been crafted separately from the rest of the foot.

At last, after minutes of effort, she succeeded in pulling the frog out of the rest of Glory's foot, like a cork out of a bottle!

Joy gasped in excitement. "His foot's *hollow!*"

"Right." Nancy probed inside with her fingers and extracted a tightly rolled brown-paper package. When unrolled, it proved to contain a handful of small, glittering gems wrapped in several sheets of letter paper that bore a man's handwriting.

"These stones," Nancy went on, turning them over to Police Chief McGinnis and Arno Franz, "are, of course, the diamonds that Fingers Malone stole at the park in St. Louis twenty years ago. And these sheets of paper are a letter to Joy from her father."

Silence settled over the room as Joy read the letter. Her eyes were misting as she handed the sheets to Nancy, one by one. The first page began:

Joy dear,

This is the hardest letter I have ever had to write. For years I could never decide whether or not to tell you the truth about your mother and the unhappy early days of our marriage. Now I have decided to leave it up to fate.

I have devised a riddle, involving your mother's name, Iris. If you are interested enough and really determined to solve the riddle in order to find out more about her, you may eventually discover this letter. If not, perhaps it is just as well that you never learn the sad truth about our past. As I say, I leave the outcome up to fate . . .

After reading the entire letter, Nancy turned to Joy. "Shall I tell the others what your father says?"

The redheaded heiress blinked and nodded, unable to speak because of her tearful emotion.

Nancy explained to the others that John Trent's wife Iris had come from a wealthy family in the Midwest, who strongly opposed her marriage to a poor, working-class machinist from a blue-collar background. Nevertheless, the two were so deeply in love that Iris had eloped with him. As a result, she became estranged from her parents.

"At first, the two newlyweds were very happy," Nancy went on. "But after their baby was born, Iris became gravely ill. The one chance to save her life was by an expensive operation that would cost thousands of dollars—far more than John Trent could raise or borrow. So, reluctantly, he was forced to turn to her parents for help. They agreed to pay for her medical care—but only if he promised to get out of her life forever."

"That shows you what mean, hardhearted people they were!" Joy's Aunt Selma blurted angrily.

"It seems so to us now," Nancy said with a sigh, "but no doubt they, too, were very unhappy over their daughter's plight. Anyhow, John finally and sadly agreed to their demands. But when he left, he took the baby with him—and covered his tracks by changing his name from Tobin to Trent."

Later, his letter said, he learned that his wife had undergone a series of delicate operations, which saved her life but left her a permanent invalid. During her few remaining months she had had to be kept on a life-support system, so that he was never able to communicate with her, even secretly.

"From that time on," Nancy ended, "John Trent suffered bitterly from feelings of guilt, wondering if he had done the right thing."

Joy, who was deeply moved by at last learning about her mother, murmured, "Oh, how I wish I could have known her! I don't even have a picture of her!"

Nancy smiled at the girl. "Perhaps not. But you do have someone who looks very much like her."

Again, Joy stared at the teenage sleuth. "I—I don't understand. What do you mean?"

Instead of replying, Nancy opened the door and beckoned to someone waiting outside. An attractive woman with dark reddish-brown hair walked into the room.

"This is Mrs. Rose Harrod," Nancy announced to the wide-eyed girl, "your mother's twin sister!"

Joy uttered a cry of astonishment. Mrs. Harrod, who by now had completely recovered from her kidnapping ordeal, came toward her, smiling and with outstretched arms, and gathered her into a fond embrace. "Oh, Joy dear! I've been trying so long and so hard to find you!"

It was a highly emotional moment. Both Rose Harrod and Joy were soon weeping tears of happiness. Rose then filled in the missing parts of the story.

She, too, like her sister Iris, had become estranged from her harsh aristocratic parents because they disapproved of her marriage. Rose's husband, then a sergeant but now a major in the U.S. Marine Corps, was currently on sea duty. But seven or eight years ago, while he was stationed in Japan, a friend had sent Rose a magazine clipping in full color, with a scribbled notation: *Doesn't this little girl look just like you did at her age!*

The picture, which seemed to have been clipped from some industrial publication or trade journal, showed an unnamed business executive buying a carousel horse for his little daughter.

"It wasn't until much later," Rose Harrod told Joy, "that I realized the little girl in the picture must be Iris's child. You see, I was out of touch with my parents and somehow lost touch with your mother, so I never learned the full story of your mother's marriage or how she came to be separated from your father."

After Rose's parents died, however, she did learn the full story and decided to trace Iris's lost daughter. Unfortunately, the clipping included no caption, and she was unable to find out what magazine it had come from.

"Then I read in the paper about the haunted carousel," Rose went on. "I saw the name on it—the *Wonderland Gallop*—and I suddenly realized it was the same merry-go-round shown in the clipping."

Accordingly, Rose had come to River Heights and talked to Leo Novak. Novak, prompted by his own greed and suspicious nature, had jumped to the conclusion that she was really after the valuable horse carved by Walter Kruse. So he deliberately misled her, pretending he had had no connection with the carousel at the time the picture was taken.

Instead, he had turned over her name and address to Fingers and Baldy. They had kidnapped Mrs. Harrod, hoping to extort any clues she might have to the whereabouts of the missing carousel horse.

Before this happened, however, Rose had gone to the River Heights Chamber of Commerce and shown them the magazine clipping. They had immediately recognized the man in the picture as the late, local machine-tool tycoon, John Trent.

After thus finally tracing her dead sister's

spouse, Rose had gone to the Trent house, trying to meet Joy—only to be painfully rebuffed by Mrs. Yawley. She had then turned to Nancy for help.

"But I did so very cautiously, as you know, Nancy," Rose Harrod added with a rueful smile. "I wasn't sure whose side you might be on."

"The real choice, I believe," said a man's voice, "now lies with Miss Joy Trent herself."

All eyes turned to the speaker, a white-haired man who had entered the room quietly behind Mrs. Harrod. He was John Trent's lawyer.

"What exactly do you mean, Mr. Trimble?" Joy asked him.

"I mean, my dear, do you prefer to place yourself under the care of your father's sister, Mrs. Selma Yawley—or your mother's sister, Mrs. Rose Harrod?"

"Now just a minute!" Mrs. Yawley cut in shrilly. "This child is not mature enough to make such a decision herself! Let me remind you that John's will names *me* as Joy's guardian!"

"Only temporarily and conditionally, madam," the attorney corrected her. "It so happens my late client, John Trent, left a codicil to his will which you have never seen."

As he spoke, Mr. Trimble extracted a paper

from his briefcase and handed it to Mrs. Yawley.

"As you will see there," he went on, "Mr. Trent realized that you and Joy might not get along well. He also foresaw that if Joy solved the riddle which he left her, she might eventually meet her mother's twin sister. He therefore added the codicil stating that, if this happened, Joy could decide for herself whether you or her other aunt should be her guardian until she comes of age."

With a glad cry, Joy rushed into Rose Harrod's embrace. Brilliant flashes blazed in the playroom as reporter Rick Jason raised his camera and began snapping photos.

For a fleeting moment, Nancy wondered if her next mystery would be as exciting as this one. She would know very soon when she accepted the challenge of the *Enemy Match*.

Her blue eyes twinkled as she whispered to Ned, "Those two crooks, Fingers and Baldy, will still have to stand trial, but I think *one* case, at least, has just been settled out of court!"

NANCY DREW® MYSTERY STORIES By Carolyn Keene